Lizzy was still shaking from her close call.

T. D. Waters. She'd gotten only a startling glimpse of the cowboy behind the wheel. But it had been plenty to recognize Agent T. D. Waters from the photo and dossier she'd been given on him.

He was now considered a rogue agent.

She definitely had to be more careful. Especially dealing with an agent like T. D. Waters. She'd heard stories about Waters. Everyone had. But few had met the man. She'd known from his dossier that he was young, just a few years older than her, and famous for completing nearly impossible assignments.

How could someone with such a reputation for bravery and dedication to his country go rogue?

USA TODAY Bestselling Author

B.J. DANIELS

WINCHESTER CHRISTMAS WEDDING

TORONTO • NEW YORK • LONDON
AMSTERDAM • PARIS • SYDNEY • HAMBURG
STOCKHOLM • ATHENS • TOKYO • MILAN • MADRID
PRAGUE • WARSAW • BUDAPEST • AUCKLAND

This book is for Lee Demarias, with special thanks to Paul Kunze for his expertise in blowing things up.

ISBN-13: 978-0-373-74567-8

WINCHESTER CHRISTMAS WEDDING

This edition published by arrangement with Harlequin Books S.A.

For questions and comments about the quality of this book please contact us at Customer_eCare@Harlequin.ca.

www.eHarlequin.com

Printed in U.S.A.

ABOUT THE AUTHOR

USA TODAY bestselling author B.J. Daniels wrote her first book after a career as an award-winning newspaper journalist and author of thirty-seven published short stories. Since then she has won numerous awards, including a career achievement award for romantic suspense and many nominations and awards for best book.

Daniels lives in Montana with her husband, Parker, and two springer spaniels, Spot and Jem. When she isn't writing, she snowboards, camps, boats and plays tennis.

To contact her, write to B.J. Daniels, P.O. Box 1173, Malta, MT 59538 or email her at bjdaniels@mtintouch.net. Check out her website at www.bjdaniels.com.

Books by B.J. Daniels

HARLEQUIN INTRIGUE

996—SECRET OF DEADMAN'S COULEE†
1002—THE NEW DEPUTY IN TOWN†
1024—THE MYSTERY MAN OF WHITEHORSE†
1030—CLASSIFIED CHRISTMAS†
1053—MATCHMAKING WITH A MISSION†
1059—SECOND CHANCE COWBOY†
1083—MONTANA ROYALTY†
1125—SHOTGUN BRIDE*
1131—HUNTING DOWN THE HORSEMAN*
1137—BIG SKY DYNASTY*
1155—SMOKIN' SIX-SHOOTER*
1161—ONE HOT FORTY-FIVE*
1198—GUN-SHY BRIDE**
1204—HITCHED!**
1210—TWELVE-GAUGE GUARDIAN**
1234—BOOTS AND BULLETS††
1240—HIGH-CALIBER CHRISTMAS††
1246—WINCHESTER CHRISTMAS WEDDING

†Whitehorse, Montana
*Whitehorse, Montana: The Corbetts
**Whitehorse, Montana: Winchester Ranch
††Whitehorse, Montana: Winchester Ranch Reloaded

CAST OF CHARACTERS

T. D. Waters—When the cowboy rode into the Winchester Ranch, the last thing he expected was a cowgirl on a fast horse and a secret that could get them both killed.

Elizabeth "Lizzy" Calder—She'd spent many summers at the McCormick Ranch—just down the road from the Winchester Ranch—never knowing the truth.

Pepper Winchester—The matriarch knew more about what was going on than she let on. But still there was a nasty surprise in store for her.

McCall Winchester—She hoped her Christmas wedding to game warden Luke Crawford at Winchester Ranch would go off without a hitch, but had her doubts.

Janie McCormick—She had her own reasons for wanting the Winchesters to pay.

Anne McCormick—With her mother in prison, she had come home to sell the ranch. Or was she also interested in revenge against the Winchesters?

Hunt McCormick—When he was seventeen, he promised his heart to a beautiful sixteen-year-old girl. He also promised to one day find her again.

Enid Hoagland—The irascible housekeeper had her own agenda, and if everyone knew what was good for them, they wouldn't try to change it.

Prologue

TD Waters nudged the man on the ground with his boot. Getting no response, he quickly turned his gaze to the horizon. The second man was just topping a rise, out of target range and too far away to give chase.

Waters cursed, shoving back his Stetson and holstering his weapon as he watched the man get away with half a million dollars. He'd lost the money—and let one of them escape.

"Where's the money?" Ace demanded as he came running up after the wild chase across the desert.

Waters pointed at the horizon just as the second drug runner was about to disappear over it.

"Shoot the bastard," Ace shouted and shoved a rifle into his hands.

Waters took aim—just as he had as a boy growing up in Montana hunting deer. He squeezed off a shot an instant before the image on the horizon disappeared.

"You got him." Ace slapped him on the back as he took the rifle back. "You are one hell of a shot, Waters. Let's go get the money and let someone else clean up this mess," he said, moving past the body on the ground.

They hadn't gone but a half-dozen yards when he heard the shots. As Ace stumbled and fell facedown in the desert sand, TD swung around, his weapon appearing in his hand as naturally as breathing.

He got off two shots before the man on the ground could fire a third shot, but by then it was too late. Ace lay dead and TD was bleeding like a stuck pig. He hadn't even realized he'd been hit.

In the distance he heard the backup plane coming in. He stumbled across the desert to the hill where he'd taken the shot at the second man. The moment he topped the rise, he saw there was no body lying in the sand. The man had gotten away, but TD had wounded him.

There was blood splattered on the money case that lay in the sand. He stepped over to it, noticing that the clasp had broken. The man had opened it and yet left it behind? With the barrel of his gun and a bad feeling settling into the pit of his stomach, he carefully lifted the lid.

Stacks of cut newsprint.

TD staggered at the implications of what he was seeing. His gaze blurred and suddenly he was aware of how badly he was bleeding. His shirt was soaked where he'd caught the bullet in his side and now droplets darkened the sand around him. All that was keeping him on his feet was his anger.

As he heard the plane coming in for a landing, he looked out across the desert. He'd wounded the second man, but hadn't killed him. The only sign of him were his footprints in the sand as they disappeared into the vast desert.

Chapter One

Three weeks later

The call woke TD Waters from a restless sleep. He glanced at the clock and swore as the phone rang again. Who the hell would be calling this time of the night?

He considered ignoring it, thinking it had to be his boss, although he couldn't imagine why Roger Collins would be calling him. The last time they'd talked he'd told Collins what he thought of his latest sting operation.

"We had our reasons for what we did," his boss said.

"You got Ace killed and for what?" TD had demanded. "That whole operation was nothing but a setup. Were you trying to get the two of us killed?"

"Don't be ridiculous," Collins had shot back.

But TD couldn't help the feeling that he'd

hit too close to home. Something had been very wrong with that entire assignment.

"Take some time off," his boss had said, getting to his feet and dismissing not only TD—but his concerns, as well. "Time to heal, relax, rethink things."

Rethink things? "Don't you mean quit asking questions? Quit voicing my suspicions?"

"I mean *heal,*" Collins said. "Even if you hadn't been wounded during the operation, you're not ready mentally to be on the job. Take a vacation. Go somewhere warm. Get some sun. We'll talk in a few more weeks."

Get some sun. Yeah, right. The truth was TD wasn't sure he'd have a job in a few weeks. And even if he did, he wasn't sure he trusted Roger Collins anymore. This wasn't the first time that he'd wondered about some of the covert operations he'd been sent on—or about Roger Collins.

TD couldn't shake the feeling that neither he nor Ace had been expected to come out of the last one alive. Was that because Ace, too, had been questioning Roger's leadership?

That's just guilt talking, he thought as he reached for the phone. He'd gotten an agent killed. He should have checked the man on the ground for a pulse. Instead he'd given him a perfunctory nudge with his boot toe, his mind on the man getting away with what he'd believed was half a million dollars of federal money.

"Waters," he said into the phone out of habit.

Silence. No, not silence. He could make out what sounded like wind in the background, a strange static on the line as if the call was coming from some place in the sticks.

The static reminded him of a sound he hadn't heard since he was eight—that eerie howl the wind made as it whipped across the eaves of an old farmhouse in the middle of nowhere.

"Hello?" he said, unable to keep the sharp edge of anxiety out of his voice.

"I'm not sure I have the right number. Were you born on May 22, 1983?" asked a clearly disguised voice. With that and the static on the line, he couldn't be sure if it was a man or a woman.

"Who is this?" he demanded as he sat up ignoring the sudden pain in his side.

"A friend."

"I doubt that."

"I have some information for you."

TD sat up straighter. "What kind of information?"

"Information about who you really are."

What? If this was some kind of joke, he was in no mood for it. He glanced toward his weapon lying within reach. He knew who he was, but apparently the caller didn't. "I don't have the time or patience for this."

He started to hang up when the voice on the other end of the line said, "I will give you information about your birth parents if you're interested."

His *birth* parents? Boy, did this guy have the wrong number. "What's in it for you?"

A slight hesitation on the other end of the line, then, "Fifty thousand dollars."

Now he knew the call had been a mistake. If his caller knew anything about him, then he would know better than to try to extort money from him.

"I know all about your home birth, the adoption and why you were given up. What's that worth to you?"

TD was shaking his head. The caller should have done his homework. He'd gotten the wrong man in more ways than one. "Sorry, but I wasn't adopted."

A dry, rattling chuckle. "Whoever told you those people who raised you in that farm-house outside of Whitehorse, Montana, were your real parents lied to you. I don't know why they were murdered, but I have a feeling you do."

He felt an odd prickle at the nape of his neck. The caller knew about the farmhouse outside Whitehorse? Knew about the murder? Collins had said he'd taken care of the past, that nothing from it would ever lead the killers to TD.

"What exactly do I get for my money?" he asked, playing along as the blood-splattered satchel full of bundled cut newspaper flashed in his mind.

"I told you, I tell you who handled the under-the-radar adoption, I tell you who your parents really are and then you can find out why they were killed. We both know you are more than capable of finding that out on your own."

TD's heart was pounding. "How do I get the money to you?"

"I'll give you a mailing address." The caller rattled off a box number in Whitehorse. "Once I have the money, I'll call you with what you need to know. I advise you to move quickly. I'm not the only one who knows who you really are. Your life is in danger. The sooner you know the truth, the better off you will be." *Click.*

TD sat holding the phone, his heart slamming against his rib cage. *What the hell?*

Grabbing his gun from the bedside table, he moved to pull back the drapes at his apartment window and look down on the deserted street. Nothing moved. No sign of life and yet he couldn't help the paranoia.

I'm going to help you disappear. Isn't that what his now boss Roger Collins had told him that day as the car he was riding in raced away from the burning farmhouse? *We can't let whoever killed your parents find out you're still alive.*

But had Roger Collins been protecting TD or the agency? Or himself?

TD had a feeling that Roger Collins would do anything to protect his position with the agency. He'd said his climb to the top had been hard. How many people had he sacrificed to get there?

TD felt the room suddenly go cold. Someone knew who he was. That is, who he had been.

He checked the call that had come in, surprised that it wasn't blocked. Whoever had called wasn't a pro. Far from it.

Jotting down the unfamiliar number, he dug out the phone book and looked up the area code. His pulse jumped. Montana?

Hurriedly, he dialed the number. The line began to ring. It rang twice more before what sounded like an old woman answered.

"Winchester Ranch."

"Someone just called me from there."

"Well, it wasn't me," she snapped. "It's after midnight. Call back tomorrow."

"Wait! Who else is there who might have called me?"

"How should I know? They come and go around here like it's a damned bus station. I'm just the housekeeper and cook. No one tells me anything."

He was afraid she would hang up. "Just tell me this. What's your nearest town?"

"Whitehorse." She did hang up, slamming down the phone.

He winced and started to call back, but stopped himself. Back at the apartment window, he studied the quiet Atlanta street again. He tried to stay calm, to think rationally.

Swearing, he closed the drapes. He'd been told all record of his life before the age of eight had been erased to protect him. Unless he wanted to end up like his parents, Collins had told him, he should forget the past. What was there in his past that even Collins didn't want him to know?

TD closed his eyes, seeing himself at eight, turning around in the back seat of the large, dark SUV as it raced away from the burning farmhouse. Inside the house were his slain parents. At least the people he had believed were his parents.

Doubt pierced through his memory, exposing what he hadn't questioned at eight, but couldn't ignore now. His parents had lived an isolated life outside of Whitehorse, Montana, in the middle of nowhere. His mother had homeschooled him. They didn't seem to have any relatives, or friends for that matter. And both had been killed—execution style, he now realized.

"Better to let the killers believe you died in that fire as well as your parents," he'd been told as he was hustled out to the waiting car. "Don't worry. Someone is taking care of everything."

That person was waiting in the car. Roger Collins. As head of a secret government agency, Collins had seen that TD was issued a new birth certificate and given a new identity. Thomas Daniel Waters was born that day. Collins had even found people to take care of him until he was old enough to be on his own, friends of his, Collins had said.

Yes, Collins had taken care of everything,

from that day at the farmhouse through college graduation and a job with his exclusive covert agency.

TD raked a hand through his hair. The stitches in his side hurt like hell. But that was nothing compared to the doubts surging through him. If Collins had taken care of everything, then why was someone calling him from Winchester Ranch near Whitehorse, Montana, saying they knew even more about him?

The caller had known his real birth date: May 22, 1983. Not the one Collins had given him: June 5, 1983. The caller had also known about the farmhouse and the deaths of his parents.

Hell, the caller seemed to know more about him than he did himself. Even TD didn't know exactly where he'd been born.

He shook his head, trying to clear out the doubts. But they had stuck. His parents had been older, neither had resembled him and he'd never really known what his father did for a living. Whatever it was, it had brought Roger Collins into his life that horrible day when he was eight.

His father must have worked for Collins. That was the only thing that made any sense now. Why hadn't he realized that before?

What if the caller was right and the Clarksons weren't his biological parents?

TD couldn't believe the route his thoughts were taking. Was he really going to believe the word of some anonymous caller in the middle of the night? He pulled out an untraceable cell phone and made the call to the number he'd been given for emergencies only.

"You have a leak. Someone knows who I am," he said without preamble.

Hesitation, then Collins said, "That's not possible."

"I just got a call. The person seems to know more about me than even I do. You said my past was erased and that not even you knew the truth. Well, someone sure as hell does."

The silence this time had a weight to it. "Sit tight. I'll have someone there in twenty minutes," Collins said.

TD hung up and looked around his small apartment. From the time he was a boy, he'd relied on his instincts. Those instincts told him he was now on his own. At eight, he'd believed the people who had killed his parents would be looking for him. Why else give him a new identity? Why else would Roger Collins treat him like his own son, get him raised and educated, and bring him into the agency?

Now TD couldn't be sure who he really had

to fear. He thought of Ace and the botched job. Ten minutes later he was packed up and gone. He'd always traveled light, knowing he might have to disappear at any moment.

By the time the sun came up, he was driving a pickup he'd paid cash for and was on his way to the Winchester Ranch somewhere near Whitehorse, Montana.

He'd tried to cover his tracks, but he knew Collins and the resources he had available to him. It was just a matter of time before he would have to deal with whoever Collins sent after him.

ROGER COLLINS CALLED IN two of his men to bring in TD Waters. He thought about sending a couple more. Waters wouldn't want to come in. Waters had been getting suspicious for some time now. He was a danger to the agency, a danger to himself. He was especially a danger to Roger Collins.

What would he do now?

Collins hated to think. He'd told the two men he'd sent to use force if necessary. He swore at the thought of how much force it would take to bring Waters in. He should have sent more men.

Thirty minutes later, he was startled out

of his thoughts when his phone rang. He snatched it up. "Did you get him?"

"He was long gone when we got here," the agent told him. "The way the place was cleaned out, I'd say he isn't planning on coming back."

Collins swore.

"He couldn't be that far ahead of us," the agent said. "We can shut down the city. He won't be able to get out."

"No." That was the last thing Collins wanted, to alert another law-enforcement agency, let alone try to shut down the city to find him. TD was too smart for that, anyway. He would have gotten rid of the big black SUV he drove courtesy of the government.

"Come back in," Collins said. "I'll take care of it."

He sat for a moment after he hung up. This couldn't have happened at a worse time. First the debacle with TD's last assignment, and now some anonymous phone call in the middle of the night.

There was no reason to panic, Collins assured himself. He knew where Waters was headed. Montana. If Waters was going after the caller, then he must have some idea where the call had come from.

Within minutes Collins had Waters's phone

records and the number—and where the call had come from: Winchester Ranch. He smiled. This was going to be too easy, since right next door to that ranch, so to speak, was the McCormick Ranch.

True, it would have to be handled with the utmost of care—and not by just anyone. He needed someone he could depend on, someone who wouldn't question any order he gave, someone who knew his way around Montana.

It would have to be a new recruit, someone who had proven himself but was new enough that TD Waters didn't know the person and wouldn't suspect him. Someone who could get close to TD, watch him and at first, simply report back. But definitely someone loyal who, when it became necessary, would make sure TD Waters never left Montana alive.

Still smiling, Collins picked up the phone and dialed. "I'm sorry to bother you in the middle of the night, Elizabeth, but I have an assignment for you that can't wait."

Chapter Two

Twelve hours later

“Lizzy?” Anne McCormick looked shocked to see her. “What are you doing here?”

Elizabeth “Lizzy” Calder hadn’t known what kind of reception she would get at the McCormick Ranch this close to Christmas—especially showing up unannounced. Fortunately she had the perfect excuse—she was here to see her childhood friend.

“I had to come, Anne,” she said honestly. “You’ve been in my thoughts ever since I heard about your mother. I am so sorry. I came as soon as I could.” Anne’s mother, Joanna McCormick, had been arrested for murder and, after making a deal for her life, had been sent to Montana state prison.

“I’m sure you were devastated when you heard,” Anne said stiffly. “More likely you weren't in the least bit surprised. We both know you never liked my mother."

Lizzy couldn't lie—at least about that. Joanna McCormick had been one of those cold, distant people who had ice water running through her veins. It had come as no surprise when she'd heard Joanna had committed a murder.

"Your mother and I weren't close, but you know I care about you," Lizzy said honestly. "How are you doing?"

Anne shook her head, then burst into tears. Lizzy stepped to her, hugging her friend. She did care about Anne. That much of the visit wasn't a lie. They were childhood friends and had once been very close.

"I'm so sorry."

"Oh, Lizzy, it's just been horrible."

"Tell me what I can do."

As her friend drew back from the hug, she smiled through her tears. "I wish there was something someone *could* do. But I am glad you're here anyway."

Lizzy tried not to show her relief. Anne hadn't been happy to see her. There had been the chance that she would turn her away, especially this close to Christmas and considering the fact that the two of them had drifted apart.

While she was sincere in her concern for her friend, Lizzy had a job to do and she never let anything get in the way of that. She'd worked too hard to get where she was, and she owed too much to Roger Collins and the agency. And right now she needed to stay here because of the ranch's proximity to the Winchester Ranch—and hopefully to TD Waters, if that was really where he'd been gone.

Leaving her travel bags at the bottom of the stairs, Lizzy and Anne moved into the once familiar living room. It had been redecorated since Lizzy had been here last. All the leather, wood and antler furnishings had been replaced with light-colored fabrics and white wicker. The room felt cold, like the day outside where a half foot of snow covered the ground and only a weak December sun shone through the window.

"Is Janie home, as well?" Lizzy asked of Anne's younger sister.

"She just arrived this morning."

The three of them couldn't have been more different. Anne, blonde and blue-eyed and chubby. Janie, small and dark. Lizzy, redheaded, gray-eyed, tall and gangly. Their appearances were only the tip of the iceberg in their differences. Anne was quiet and easygoing, Janie moody and volatile, and Lizzy…

well, she had been the wild one when they were kids. Up for anything.

That was how she'd broken her arm after falling out of the barn's hayloft. She had loved being daring, especially when it came to riding horses. The faster the better was her motto. She remembered how her father used to worry about her when he'd see her racing across the prairie on one of the ranch horses.

Lizzy took a seat in one of the wicker chairs, wishing for the old, deep leather couch that she and Anne used to curl up in to giggle and talk, eat popcorn and watch old Westerns.

As she looked around, she yearned for something familiar in the room. She didn't want to believe that everything had changed here, not at what had once been her most favorite place in the world.

With a start, she saw that the old framed photographs that had covered the far wall were gone. They'd been replaced with a huge, ugly piece of modern artwork.

"What happened to the photographs?" she asked in alarm. There'd been photos of her father and Anne's stepfather, Hunt, along with Lizzy and Anne as girls and even black-and-white snapshots of long-ago visitors to the ranch.

Anne shrugged. "Probably in the basement." Her look said she wondered why Lizzy would care. "You can help yourself to any you want. They'll probably get thrown out after we leave."

"Thank you." Lizzy looked at her friend and felt her heart go out to her. "You won't be staying at the ranch then?"

Anne shook her head. "Janie and I are selling the place. Mother's signed it over to us."

The thought broke her heart. "What about your dad?"

"Hunt's my stepfather," Anne said, a warning in her tone. "Unfortunately, Mother never divorced him, but he said he doesn't want any of the money so I guess that is something."

Lizzy didn't think she could hurt any worse. She hated that Anne, and she was sure Janie, felt this way about the man who had been the only father either of them had known. Joanna had been married twice before to two other men. None had lasted, leaving behind three children, Jordan, Anne and Janie.

"I'm sorry to hear that," Lizzy said. "About the ranch and the way you feel about Hunt." She'd loved Hunt like a second father. And she'd heard it was Joanna who'd refused to divorce Hunt—not the other way around even though they had lived apart for years now.

"I told you," Anne said with an edge to her voice, "things have changed around here."

She nodded, unable to speak. So much had changed after her father died—like summers at the McCormick Ranch. He'd been the ranch manager and best friends with Hunt. Anne had been like the sister she'd never had—at least during the summers. The rest of the year they'd all been away at different boarding schools.

Lizzy had lived for her summers when she could get back to the ranch, her father, her friend and the horses she loved. She and Anne spent long days horseback riding, not just around the McCormick Ranch, but sneaking onto the even larger Winchester Ranch to the northwest.

It had been a game, seeing how close they could get to the Winchester Ranch lodge, terrified that Pepper Winchester might see them and…well, they'd heard stories about how mean she was and had no idea what she might do.

Lizzy's father, Will, had loved this ranch and had worked it until he died. Her happiest memories were here. As she looked around the room, she could no longer imagine her father—or any other ranch hand for that matter—in this room.

As her gaze settled again on Anne, she tried to accept that a lot more had changed than just the furnishings. Including Lizzy's real reason for coming here.

"I'm glad your sister is here with you," she said to fill the uncomfortable silence. Since college and her father's death, Lizzy hadn't seen as much of Anne. At first they'd kept in touch through emails and phone calls, but even those had been scarce the past few years. "How is Janie doing?"

Anne glanced toward the stairs and lowered her voice. "I'm worried about her. You know how close she and Mother were."

As close as Joanna McCormick could be to any human being, Lizzy thought. Joanna loved horses and hadn't seemed to have any love left over for her husband and her children. "I'm sorry."

She knew firsthand what it was like to lose a parent. She'd lost her mother at the age of three. All she knew about the pretty woman from the photographs her father had shown her was that her father had loved his wife more than life.

"If I hadn't had you," he used to say. "You were my reason to go on living."

Lizzy still missed her father desperately. Was that another reason she'd jumped at the chance to join the agency? Roger Collins had said it was like a family. That's why she had been excited about coming back here for this assignment. This had once been home.

"I wish you had called before coming, though," Anne said. "As much as I appreciate it, I'm afraid you being here will upset Janie."

"What will upset Janie?" asked a voice from the stairs.

They both turned to see Anne's younger sister standing halfway down the steps. Janie was still small, wiry, with dark hair and eyes like her mother. Even though Anne hadn't been Hunt's child, she resembled him.

The thought startled Lizzy. Was it possible Anne and Janie had different fathers? And why hadn't she thought of that before, since the sisters were so different in every way? After all, Anne and Janie's older brother, Jordan, had had a different father than his half sisters. Jordan had died in a ranching accident before Lizzy was born.

"Why would a visit from my sister's friend upset me?" Janie asked smiling as she came down the stairs to give Lizzy a hug.

"You look great, Janie," she said and then realized how that must sound. Unlike Anne, Janie *did* look great. Anne's skin was pale with dark shadows under lifeless eyes. Janie was radiant, eyes almost too bright.

"My sister and I mourn losses very differently," Janie said, crossing the room to hug her sister. Anne looked as surprised by Janie's show of affection as Lizzy had been. Neither of them believed it was real, she thought uncharitably.

"So how long are you staying?" Janie asked. Before Liz could answer, Janie rushed on. "Stay through the holidays," she said impulsively. "It will be just like old times, won't it, Anne?"

Lizzy saw a look pass between the sisters. She opened her mouth to say she wasn't sure how long she would be staying, but this time Anne cut her off.

"I'm sure Lizzy isn't staying that long," her old friend said pointedly. "After all, she has a job. I'm sorry, I've forgotten what you said you do."

"I'm a consultant for companies planning to expand," Liz said, giving her the practiced spiel.

"How horribly boring," Janie chimed in with a laugh. "I'm sure they can get along without you for a while. I mean, how many companies are expanding in this poor economy? I'll tell Alma we have a guest so she can add another plate." She headed for the kitchen humming to herself.

"We should get you settled into the guest room," Anne said, abruptly getting to her feet.

It wasn't until they'd carried Lizzy's bags up the stairs to the guest wing that Anne spoke again. "You see why I'm worried about her? She's taking all of this much worse than she's letting on. I'm afraid of what she's going to do."

"Do?"

Anne didn't answer, but Liz had a bad feeling it involved the Winchesters and that old rumor about Anne's stepfather, Hunt, and Pepper Winchester.

"I need to see to some things," Anne said distractedly. "Make yourself at home."

There was only one thing that could make Lizzy feel at home here. She changed and headed for the stables. The Winchester Ranch was only a few miles away—if you went across the country the way a bird flies—and it was time she got to work.

PEPPER WINCHESTER HAD BEEN more than a little surprised when her son Worth showed up at the ranch for the wedding days early. She hadn't even been that sure he was coming for the wedding. She'd never understood Worth. Nor him her.

"I need to talk to you," he said now as he stepped into the parlor and closed the door behind him.

She'd been reading quietly in front of the fire, but now she put her book aside, seeing that he had something on his mind. She watched him fidget nervously and felt her stomach tighten. Whatever it was wasn't anything good.

"I know your secret," he blurted out, avoiding her gaze. "I know the real reason you were a recluse the past twenty-seven years."

She said nothing.

He finally looked up, his eyes locking with hers for the first time in years. "I need money. I need you to give it to me."

Pepper Winchester studied her son, astonished. After all these years he'd finally grown a backbone?

"You aren't really blackmailing me, are you?" she asked amused.

"I'm serious."

"I can see that." Pepper thought of her long-dead husband, Call. He would have been as shocked as she was to see Worth—or "Worthless" as Call had always referred to him—standing here making demands.

He looked away. "I wouldn't ask except…"

"You're desperate. Gambling? Drugs? High-priced call girls?"

Worth shook his head angrily. "Don't make fun of me."

"I was merely asking what put you in such a…dire predicament that your only option was to blackmail your mother."

"I'm so glad you find this amusing," he said, anger reddening his cheeks. "I hope you find it as hilarious when I go public with your not-so-little secret."

She studied him for a long moment. Any other woman seventy-two years old facing a man Worth's size might have been frightened. She could see that he was desperate, that this was a last-ditch effort to save himself. But from what?

"I'll need to know where my money is going," she said.

He shook his head, his dark gaze glittering, almost with malice. "No, that's not part of the deal."

"What makes you think I will give you the money, then?"

Worth smiled. Unlike her other sons, he was even less handsome when he smiled. Of her five children, Worth was the one she'd worried about the most. He'd always had the darkest disposition, the most secretive personality. Before this moment, Pepper would have said she couldn't imagine what Worth was thinking.

"How much money are we talking?" she asked, though she had no intention of giving him a cent.

"How much of the Winchester fortune is left?"

She raised a brow.

"I know Virginia's been here for months trying to get her greedy little hands on it," Worth said. "But I assume she wouldn't still be here if you'd given her any. I want my share."

"Those were your sister's sentiments, as well." Pepper didn't tell him that Virginia had since given up her share. She wasn't sure Worth would have believed that.

It saddened her to see the job she and Call had done with their offspring. Some people shouldn't have been allowed to have children, she thought, then thought of her grandchildren and couldn't imagine not having known them.

"What have you been doing all these years for a living?" she asked.

He sneered. "Now you're interested? Where were you the past twenty-seven years? Oh, that's right, hiding out here on the ranch. Repenting for your sins?" His laugh had a sharp, lethal edge to it. "Not likely, huh?"

"I heard you have a good business," she said, unaffected by his attitude or his snide remarks. "Where did all that money go, since I know you never married, never had children." That might have been a blessing in disguise, she realized now.

Worth merely glared at her. "If you want to play games, I will take a certified check for one-fifth of the market value of this ranch." He reached into his pocket and took out a piece of paper. "This is my share of what what I estimate it's worth." He tossed the scrap of paper on the end table. "I'll need that check now."

She glanced at the scrap of paper and the amount written on it. So like Worth to settle for less, she thought. "I'd like to have my own appraisal done, if you don't mind," she said, stalling.

Worth looked panicked and she wondered just what kind of trouble he was in. Something serious.

"I should be able to give it to you after McCall's wedding."

He started to argue, but she held up her hand.

"Otherwise, you can take your blackmail and—"

"Fine," he snapped, looking defeated, before storming out.

Leaning on her cane, Pepper got up and tossed the scrap of paper into the fire. She watched it burn, thinking that her children continued to surprise her.

And she them, she thought, although they didn't know it yet.

TD WATERS FELT AS IF he'd been driving for hours on the narrow, snowy road into wild remote country. Since leaving Whitehorse, Montana, he hadn't seen another vehicle.

The land was familiar, wide-open, snow-covered prairie that ran as far as the eye could see. He'd passed only a few farmhouses, cattle dark against the winter landscape, and then nothing but sagebrush and rocky outcroppings studded with a few stunted junipers.

He couldn't help but think of the remote farmhouse where he'd grown up—not that far from the Winchester Ranch. The problem with this part of the Missouri Breaks badlands was the lack of roads. The farmhouse where he'd spent his first eight years of life was on the other side of a deep ravine closer to what was known as Old Town Whitehorse.

He hadn't thought of his childhood in years—at least the first eight years of it—and didn't want to now. With his mother homeschooling him and the nearest house miles away, his only friend had been his dog. But he'd enjoyed the country and he liked to think that those hours spent exploring and being alone with his thoughts had made him strong, independent and capable of taking care of himself.

It crossed his mind that he was taking one hell of a chance coming back here. If anything Roger Collins had told him was true, then his life could be in danger—just as his late-night caller had warned him. Coming back here could also be a suicide mission if he started digging into the past—and Collins was determined to stop him.

He also questioned his impulsive decision to just appear on the doorstep of the Winchester Ranch. But it was the only lead he had. If his caller's plan had been to lure him to Montana and the Winchester Ranch, it had worked like a charm.

TD knew that he probably wasn't thinking clearly. He was still recovering from his gunshot wound—and Ace's death. Maybe worse was that nagging suspicion that Ace wasn't the only one who was supposed to die that day and that he could no longer trust his boss—the man who had allegedly saved him almost twenty years ago.

He couldn't shake the feeling that he'd been lied to about who he was and how he'd ended up working for Roger Collins. The whole mess made him angry and feeling the need to butt some heads. His late-night caller would do for a start.

TD didn't like being jerked around. He would find out who was behind it—or die trying.

With relief, he saw that he'd finally reached the turnoff to the ranch. He swung the pickup under a large log arch that read *Winchester Ranch* and started down an even narrower snowy road.

Suddenly TD caught movement coming at him fast from the right. He hit the brakes. Snow filled the air, then he saw the flash of horseflesh—and the woman straddling the horse. She appeared for only an instant, a vision on a huge, powerful chestnut mare. Her long auburn hair blew back in a wave from under the Western hat. Her face was flushed, her light-colored eyes wide with what he'd taken for both surprise and excitement as her horse came down in the middle of the road and bounded up in one smooth, graceful leap to the opposite side of the narrow road.

As his pickup slid to a stop, his heart in his throat, she disappeared over a rise as if he'd only imagined her.

"What the hell?" he cursed as he gripped the wheel. That had been way too close for comfort. The fool woman could have been killed.

He waited, expecting her to come back and apologize for scaring the hell out of him. But she didn't return.

After a moment, he got the pickup going again, replaying the scene in his memory, seeing the woman and horse flying through the air. She damned sure could ride!

He recalled her face, her expression, and felt a chill. That split-second when their gazes had locked, he'd originally taken her look as shock. It had been shock all right. She had recognized him.

Driving up the road, he knew whatever else he came here to accomplish, he had to find that woman.

Chapter Three

Sheriff McCall Winchester felt herself getting more anxious as Christmas and her wedding date approached. It was going to be tense enough just putting her grandmother and mother together.

While they seemed to have called a truce, there was a lot of history there, all of it bad. McCall could only hope for the best when it came to throwing Pepper and Ruby together.

But when she added the rest of the family to the mix, it felt like a powder keg. All it would take was one spark to set the whole thing off. She knew anything could happen—and probably would.

When the sheriff's department dispatcher called back to her office to say that Cyrus Winchester would like to see her, she said to send him back. She hoped there wasn't a problem, but with her family there usually was.

McCall suspected wedding bells would be

ringing soon for Cyrus and Kate Landon, the owner of Secondhand Kate's, the used furnishings emporium in town.

Her cousin Cyrus had left Whitehorse just long enough to make arrangements to sell his share of the private investigating business he used to run with his twin brother, Cordell, in Denver.

"Hi, coz," Cyrus said as he came through the door. Like all the Winchesters, he had the dark eyes and hair that made the whole bunch of them stand out—not to mention the fact that they often ended up the topic of gossip in Whitehorse.

"Cyrus." McCall saw his expression and had a bad feeling that, just as she'd feared, this wasn't a social call.

"I thought I'd stop by and see how the wedding plans were going."

She nodded, wishing she didn't know the Winchesters so well. "Sure you did. What's really on your mind?"

He laughed. "I forget sometimes we share the same genes. I thought you should know that the McCormick girls were back in town."

Anne and Janie McCormick. "I figured they'd come back to the ranch. Someone needs to run it now that their mother is in prison."

"Sell it, from what I've heard."

"I would have thought Hunt might come back and take the ranch over," McCall said. She'd heard rumors about her grandmother and Hunt McCormick. She'd always wondered if that had started the ill will between the families.

"From what I heard, Hunt is giving up his share of the ranch," Cyrus said. "What bothers me is the timing with your wedding and our grandmother still convinced that someone in the family conspired to have your father murdered."

McCall nodded. She had suspected for some time that it was the reason Pepper Winchester had invited her family back to the ranch over the past few months. She was looking for a killer.

"I'm not sure you know just how much our grandmother idolized her youngest son, Trace," Cyrus was saying.

She'd heard. "To the exclusion of her other children."

"Afraid so. There are some deep scars there."

"And some deep resentments. Is that what you're trying to tell me? You agree with her that one of them was a coconspirator in my father's death?"

Trace Winchester had been murdered before McCall was born, but his body hadn't been found until recently. Their grandmother, Pepper, had believed Trace Winchester had run away. She'd become a recluse for twenty-seven years, until recently, when she'd learned what had really happened.

Since the discovery of Trace's remains, one murderer had been caught. Unfortunately that killer had sworn a member of the Winchester Family had been involved. The problem was that the killer had died before giving McCall a name—and wasn't necessarily reliable when it came to the truth.

"It does seem odd that my father was killed within sight of the ranch," McCall said.

Cyrus laughed. "Don't try to con a con man. That high ridge is directly across a deep ravine from Winchester Ranch. Neither of us thinks that was a coincidence that Trace was killed there." He seemed to hesitate. "You know Grandmother believes one of her grandchildren saw the murder."

McCall said nothing.

"She found some party hats in that horrible third-floor room that Call Winchester had used to punish his children in," Cyrus continued. "The party hats were for Trace's birthday—the one he never made it to. There were five hats in that room—and a pair of binoculars."

McCall nodded, seeing why her grandmother had her suspicions. "*Five* hats?" And only three grandchildren at the ranch that day.

"I was in the room with Cordell and Jack, the nanny's son, who we now know is one of us."

That took care of her cousins. "Who else was in the room that day?" She already had a bad feeling what he was going to say.

"The two McCormick girls. They used to sneak over all the time. If Pepper had caught them on the ranch… You know how much she hated Joanna McCormick and vice versa."

McCall figured the bad blood between the family was why the girls had sneaked over all the time. Winchester Ranch would be off limits, so of course they would go there. And if they got caught? She hated to think of what her grandmother might have done to them—not to mention what Enid, the meanest housekeeper alive, would have done.

"You're saying you think one of them saw the murder?" she asked.

"All I know is that I didn't see anything and neither did Cordell, and Jack never had the binoculars."

"But the girls looked through them," she guessed. Her pulse was thundering in her ears. "Why wouldn't they have come forward or at least said something to someone?"

He shrugged. "They were very young. Maybe they didn't realize what they'd seen, especially that little one."

Janie. McCall remembered seeing her and her sister around town when they were kids. Joanna would cross the street with the girls to avoid any of the Winchesters. The McCormick girls hadn't gone to school in Whitehorse, so McCall hadn't had any contact with them. Then their mother had sent them to boarding school back east.

"There's a chance no one saw anything," McCall said. "Also that the killer was lying about a member of the family being involved." She couldn't help thinking of that night when she'd faced Sandy Sheridan. Sandy had taunted that someone in the family had pushed her into killing Trace Winchester. Was it true, though? Or had Sandy just wanted to cause more trouble for McCall's family?

She hadn't known then and she certainly didn't know now. But if it was true, then McCall had to know—and not just because she was the sheriff.

Cyrus got to his feet. "I thought you'd want

to know what was going on. You picked a hell of a time to get married out at the ranch."

Didn't she though, McCall thought as she got to her feet. "Thanks for giving me a heads-up. I guess I'll drive out to the McCormick Ranch and see how Anne and Janie are doing."

Her cousin raised a brow. "Be careful. Given the way they feel about the Winchesters, I'd watch my back if I were you."

TD DROVE OVER A HILL and below him he got his first look at the Winchester Ranch lodge. He slowed the pickup, still shaken from his near collision with the woman on the horse—and the certainty that she'd recognized him.

As the pickup rolled down the hill toward the Winchester lodge, he realized he had no idea what he was getting into. Was the redhead riding the horse from this ranch? He didn't think so, given the direction she'd gone after their close call. But maybe, he thought, as he noticed a half-dozen horses milling in a corral down by the barn.

The ranch buildings were nestled against the hillside, looking like something out of an old Western movie. At the heart of the scene was a sprawling log lodge with several wings and floors, including a third floor at the far back on what appeared to be an older wing.

The place instantly captivated him. His curiosity increased as he pulled up in the yard and an old woman opened the front door of the lodge and motioned for him to hurry up.

"It's about time," she snapped as he opened his pickup door to get out. She was broomstick thin, a wiry, withered old crone with dark, beady eyes and a turned-down mouth.

"I beg your pardon?" he asked, realizing this had to be the same person he'd spoken to when he'd called the ranch that night. Same impatience, same gravelly old voice.

"You're staying in the bunkhouse," she said, pointing to a building down by the barn. "You can park over there. But get a move on. I can't do everything myself and I need the supplies put in the pantry."

"I think there might be a mistake," he said.

"There's no mistake. You were hired to do whatever I say and I'm saying get a move on." She turned on her skinny legs and disappeared back into the lodge, slamming the door behind her.

He stared after her for a moment, considering this turn of events, then slid back behind the wheel of his pickup and drove down by the barn to the small cabin bunkhouse.

He parked the truck, looking around for a moment before going in. The bunkhouse was clean, cold and apparently vacant. Dropping his bag on one of the bottom twin beds, he turned up the heater on the wall, then glanced out toward the corral and the horses.

None matched the big chestnut mare with the blaze of white that the redhead had been riding, but then she wouldn't have returned yet—if this is where she'd come from. He didn't think she would be that hard to find. There couldn't be many close ranches out here, could there?

As he walked back up to the lodge, he wondered how long he could get away with this obvious case of mistaken identity. Maybe long enough to find out who had called him from here. But one thing was certain, he wasn't leaving Montana until he got what he came for, and now he also had a woman to track down.

LIZZY WAS STILL SHAKING from her close call. She'd galloped off a safe distance, then stopped to listen, half afraid he would come after her on foot.

TD Waters. She'd only gotten a startling

glimpse of the cowboy behind the wheel. But it had been plenty to recognize Agent TD Waters from the photo and dossier she'd been given.

Well, at least now she knew that her information had been correct. He'd come to Montana to the Winchester Ranch. All she'd been told was that he'd received a phone call from here before taking off against orders.

TD Waters was now considered a rogue agent.

Her heart was still pounding. The first time back on a horse in years and she hadn't been paying attention, unaware she'd already reached the Winchester Ranch road. It was no wonder she'd lost track of where she was with everything in the landscape blanketed in white. Not that that was an excuse.

She definitely had to be more careful. Especially dealing with an agent like TD Waters. Lizzy knew she was shaken from more than her close call. She'd heard stories about Waters. Everyone had, but few had met the man. She'd known from his dossier that he was young, just a few years older than herself, and famous for completing nearly impossible assignments.

How could someone with such a reputation

for bravery and dedication to his country go rogue?

She circled her horse back toward the Winchester Ranch, wondering what he was doing here. She'd been warned that he was dangerous and had seen something in his photograph that had given her pause.

But his photo was nothing like seeing him in the flesh. Even in that brief instant that their eyes had locked, she'd felt the intensity of his dark gaze and felt a shudder at the realization of just how dangerous this man could be.

Lizzy shivered now at the memory as she came to a small rise. When she'd been given the assignment, she hadn't been privy to why Agent TD Waters was in Montana or why he was going to the Winchester Ranch. Her assignment had been to observe, report and wait for further instructions.

She watched from a distance as he spoke for a few moments with a woman at the front door of the lodge, then drove down and parked in front of a small cabin near the barn. He carried in two large bags, one long enough at least to hold an assault rifle. She had no doubt he would be armed.

As he came back out, he headed for the main lodge again, but the same woman he'd spoken to before appeared at another door and motioned him in. Lizzy frowned. The woman was wearing an apron.

Lizzy found herself even more curious about the rogue agent. What a coincidence that he'd come to a ranch so close to where she'd spent all those summers.

Coincidence always made Agent Lizzy Calder suspicious—and on her guard. She quickly realized she was going to have to get a lot closer to the lodge—and TD Waters—if she hoped to find out what he was doing here.

In fact, now seemed like the perfect time to see what TD Waters had in those two bags he'd carried into the cabin.

TD HAD ALMOST REACHED the lodge when a door had opened off one of the wings. He'd caught a whiff of bread baking before the old woman he'd met earlier had waved him into the ranch kitchen.

"You can start by unloading all of the food into the pantry," she'd ordered. Now a door swung open behind her and another woman appeared.

He guessed this second woman was in her fifties, tall, dark-eyed, with shoulder-length black hair. She was dressed in flannel pants and a sweater.

Her gaze fell over him questioningly. She looked to the old crone who'd put him to work. "Enid?"

Enid glanced over her shoulder. "Him? He was sent out from the employment agency to help with keeping you all fed before the wedding."

"TD," he said introducing himself to the woman before he began to unload the boxes of groceries onto the pantry shelves.

"TD?"

"TD Waters."

She didn't introduce herself, simply asked what they were having for lunch and left.

"Who was that?" he asked after she was gone.

"Virginia Winchester. Acts like she owns the place. She wishes," Enid said, actually smiling. "She and her two brothers think they're going to get this ranch. They don't know their mother. Pepper'll find a way to take it with her—that's if she ever dies."

So Pepper Winchester owned the ranch, Virginia was her daughter and there were two sons. "So where is Mr. Winchester?" he asked, wondering if there was any truth to what he'd heard in town when he'd asked about the Winchesters.

"Dead." He felt her hard little eyes on him. "You must not be from around here."

"No," he admitted. He continued unloading the groceries, wondering what he was going to do when the real help arrived.

Although he was thankful he'd gotten his foot in the door, so to speak, he felt the clock ticking. He needed to find out who else was here on the ranch.

"I would imagine you have a lot of guests staying here with the wedding and all," he ventured.

"Just the family, but believe me, that's plenty." Enid struggled to lift a tray filled with four cups and a carafe of coffee.

"Here, let me take that for you."

For a moment he didn't think she was going to relinquish the tray. Their eyes met, hers bright with determination and need for power.

"They don't expect you to be carting around a heavy tray like this all the time, do they?" he asked disapprovingly, hoping he'd hit on the right note.

Enid let out a snort as she let him take the tray. "You have no idea what I have to put up with around here. I was here before Pepper showed up fresh from her honeymoon… I was just a kid myself when I started working for

Call Winchester's parents. This place feels more like mine than any of these so-called Winchesters'."

He could see she was about to take off on a tangent. "How many people do you have to wait on?" he asked, trying to get her back on track.

"Well, before all this recent nonsense it was just me, my husband—bless his soul—and Mrs. Winchester." She had stopped to cross herself and without wasting a breath continued. "Now with Pepper's three grown children hanging around..." She let out a sigh. "The two sons aren't so bad, but that daughter, Virginia..."

"I'm sorry, is your husband deceased?"

"You could say that."

"Have the others been here long?"

"Just a few days this time."

"So you haven't had any wedding guests yet," he said.

"Won't be getting any either. The wedding is family only. That will be enough of a free-for-all. There's a bunch of grandchildren coming with their significant others. We'll be lucky if someone doesn't get killed." He started to ask if she was serious, but she noticed he was still holding the tray.

She dropped a plate of stale-looking sugar

cookies onto the tray. "Better get that to them. Virginia will be having a hissy fit. The parlor is straight down the hall. Second door on the right. Make sure you don't spill anything."

"I'll do my best." He gave her a smile and said, "I'll be right back to finish the pantry."

She glanced toward it and seemed surprised how many of the boxes he'd already unloaded. "Good. Don't dally. We have a lot of work to do before lunch."

He headed down the hall, fairly certain that whoever had called him was still in this house.

CIRCLING AROUND TO COME up behind the barn, Lizzy swung down from her horse, wrapped the reins around the corral rail and slipped through to the back of the bunkhouse.

Standing in the cold shadow of the cabin, she listened. She hadn't seen anyone around the barn, hadn't heard anyone inside as she'd moved to the corner of the building. No sound from inside the bunkhouse, no other vehicle outside it other than the pickup TD Waters had been driving.

She glanced toward the house, but saw no movement. Unless someone came out of the house, they wouldn't see her slip inside the bunkhouse.

Lizzy had been over here before and remembered the lodge as being much larger, much more ominous, when she and Anne and Janie had ridden over and spied on the Winchesters.

Even then, apparently, she'd wanted to be a spy, she thought.

The wing of the house that faced this direction was old and boarded up. Lizzy remembered sneaking in through the boards over one of the broken windows to look around. It had been nothing more than empty, dusty rooms, but she recalled the old root cellar at the back. They'd found a bunch of dust-covered jars of canned goods. Janie had wanted to try the contents.

Lizzy shook her head at the memory.

She studied the house a moment longer. Still no movement. Apparently Waters wasn't coming back. At least not yet.

Lizzy moved quickly, slipping around the front and through the small cabin door. She stopped just inside, closing the door behind her. For a moment, she just let her gaze take in the interior. There were bunk beds on the wall to both her left and right. Directly in front of her was the door into a large bathroom with several shower stalls.

Waters had put his two bags on one of the bunks to the right.

She checked the window, drawing back the curtain. Coast clear. Memorizing the exact placement of the bags, she went to the bunk bed and pulled the first bag over to her. With swift efficiency, she went through it, finding nothing but clothing.

Replacing that bag, she searched the second one, listening in case she heard anyone approaching from outside. The second one held a rifle as well as several small pistols. TD had come prepared for war, apparently.

Each was wrapped in an item of clothing. She put them back as they had been, noticing something else stuck in the side of the bag. It was flat and hard and about the size of a book, and wrapped in a soft, blue T-shirt. With interest, she carefully unwrapped it.

To her surprise, it was a framed photograph of TD Waters as a boy. He was smiling at the camera, eyes dark, his Western hat pushed back to expose his young eager face. He was holding a rifle. At his feet was a large mongrel dog. The dog was looking up at the boy with such love…

She turned the cheap frame over to see that

the back of the photograph was partially exposed. She could see part of a date. Lifting the backing, she was able to read the rest: Johnny Ray Clarkson, summer 1991.

Lizzy quickly wiped her fingerprints off the frame and carefully rewrapped the photograph just as it had been. She put everything back into the bag and replaced it too just as it had been. Straightening the bedspread, she frowned to herself.

There was no doubt that the boy in the photograph was Waters. The date would have been about right. The boy in the snapshot looked to be about nine or ten. He could have been younger. Waters could have just been tall for his age. So why did it say on the back of the photo that his name was Johnny Ray Clarkson?

And why was it that the framed photograph was the only personal item Waters had brought with him? Her boss had said that Waters had cleaned out his apartment as if he wasn't returning.

She thought of the innocence of youth she'd seen in the boy's face—and compared it to the clearly dangerous man she'd seen behind the wheel of the pickup earlier and felt a twinge. Would she be like that in a few more years with the agency?

Lizzy checked the window again, then, taking one last look at the room—especially the location of the bags on the bed—she slipped out of the bunkhouse and headed for her horse—and the McCormick Ranch—anxious to call in her report.

Chapter Four

TD carried the tray down the hall. At the large living room he slowed. This place was impressive, with its gigantic rock fireplace and towering ceiling. A wide, log-railed stairway curved up to the second floor. The furnishings looked as old as the outside of the lodge, but even with his untrained eye, he could see that they had been expensive and were probably now antiques.

From what little he'd been able to find out about the ranch at an internet café on the way to Montana, the ranch was huge and Pepper Winchester eccentric and apparently quite wealthy.

He'd made a point of stopping at a café in Whitehorse. During his years at the agency, he'd found that people in small towns were more open than those in large cities. All he'd had to do was bring up the topic of the Winchesters with the young waitress when he'd asked directions to the ranch and she'd given him an earful.

"Do you know Pepper Winchester?" the waitress had asked.

"Not yet. Why?"

"Well," she said lowering her voice. "Hardly anyone has seen her in more than twenty-five years I guess. She locked herself up in that big old place years ago. I guess she only wears black." The girl shivered. "You wouldn't believe all the wild stories I've heard about her and that place."

"Like what?"

"That she killed her husband."

"Really?"

"Well, of course she said her housekeeper's husband did it." The girl had rolled her eyes. "You sure you want to go out there?" She'd laughed and gone off to fill a customer's coffee cup.

He had left the café even more curious about the Winchesters and whoever had called him from the ranch.

Now, as he reached the open parlor door, he realized he was most anxious to finally meet the infamous Pepper Winchester.

AS LIZZY RODE HER HORSE down into the McCormick ranch yard, she noticed the

Whitehorse County Sheriff patrol car parked in front of the McCormick house.

More trouble? She hoped not. One of the ranch hands offered to take care of her horse. Normally, she would insist on putting her own mount away, but she was worried about what was going on in the house.

At the front door, she slipped in and stopped at the sound of voices.

"I just need to ask you a few questions." Lizzy didn't recognize the female voice.

"What is this about, Sheriff *Winchester?*" Janie's tone was sarcastic.

"I'm not answering any questions," Anne snapped.

"Let's see what the sheriff has to say." Janie again.

"I need to ask you if you might have seen something the day Trace Winchester was murdered."

Anne let out a laugh. "You can't be serious. Why would we know anything about that, Sheriff?"

"Because you were at the Winchester Ranch that day hanging out with three of my cousins in that third-floor room that looks out on the ridge where Trace Winchester was murdered twenty-seven years ago."

"I was seven." Anne laughed again. "You

expect me to remember something from twenty-seven years ago?"

"I remember," Janie spoke up. "And I was only five."

Lizzy could well imagine the look Anne was giving her younger sister.

"What do you remember?" the sheriff asked.

"Party hats," Janie said. "But other than that…"

"The witnesses will swear that the two of you took turns looking through a pair of binoculars that morning," the sheriff said.

"Those witnesses are wrong," Anne said.

"Look, if there is any chance one of you might have witnessed the murder, I'd appreciate your help. I'm trying to find out who was on that ridge at the time of the murder."

"Sorry," Janie said. "I don't remember looking through any binoculars. If I had seen something, I might have mentioned it to my mother. You could ask her. Oh, that's right, she's in prison and it's doubtful she'd want to talk to you, now isn't it?"

"I think you should leave, Sheriff," Anne said.

Silence, then, "If either of you should change your mind, give me a call."

Lizzy stepped back into the shadows as the

sheriff left. As the front door slammed, she heard Anne explode.

"Why did you tell her we were there?" Anne demanded.

"Because we were and we both looked through the binoculars. We both saw something on that ridge."

"You're wrong," Anne said. "I didn't see anything."

Janie laughed. "Well, maybe I saw something." She had started toward the stairs when she spotted Lizzy. "Anne, your friend has been spying on us." With that she turned and ran up the stairs.

Lizzy stepped out of her hiding place, wishing she'd had the sense either to interrupt or return to the barn. "I didn't want to interrupt."

Anne waved it off. "The Winchesters are always trying to pin something on us. Don't pay any attention to Janie. If we'd seen someone get murdered, don't you think we would have told someone?"

Yes, Anne would have. But what would Janie have done? Lizzy wondered. She glanced toward the stairs and was startled to see Janie standing at the top landing watching them—and listening to what they were saying. If Janie's smile had had an edge to it earlier, now it was lethal.

"I'm sure you're right," Lizzy told Anne, even though she couldn't help but wonder if one—or both—of the McCormick sisters had seen the murder.

THE DOOR TO THE PARLOR was open, but TD still tapped on it to let the Winchesters inside know he was there.

All four of them looked up, clearly surprised to see him. The one who'd stopped by the kitchen earlier, Virginia, spoke first.

"Finally. Enid knows I have low blood sugar." She glanced at her watch. "That's probably why she sent you instead of bringing it herself."

"The tray was a little heavy for her," he said.

"Well, tell her to use the cart. She is so stubborn," Virginia said, turning to the other woman in the room. "She really is way too old for this job. I don't understand why you don't get rid of her, Mother."

"I know you don't." It was the mother's penetrating gaze TD felt on him as he stepped into the room. He guessed Pepper Winchester to be in her late sixties, possibly early seventies. She was a striking woman with salt-and-pepper dark hair plaited in a long braid that hung over one shoulder. She wore a Western shirt, jeans and moccasins—nothing black—and had an aura that clearly said she was the lady of the house.

TD wondered what else the waitress in town had gotten wrong. He knew that along with good information, you often got a lot of rumor. But he could certainly see how this woman could keep the town talking about her. There was something about her that warned him to tread carefully.

"You may put the tray down there," Pepper said, motioning to the coffee table in front of the small rock fireplace.

TD did as he was instructed, taking in the other two people in the room. Both men were dressed in Western attire. Both looked bored and sullen and barely seemed to notice him. Unlike their mother.

"I'm sorry, I don't believe we've met," Pepper said, those dark eyes boring into him.

He turned his attention back to her as she extended her hand. Her grasp was firm, her palm warm and dry.

"His name is TD," Virginia said as she reached for one of the cookies on the tray.

"TD Waters," he said to Pepper. "I'm

helping Enid." All of which was true, even if he wasn't the person she thought she'd hired.

"Would you like me to pour?" he asked, motioning to the coffee tray. His gaze was still locked with Pepper Winchester's. While what he'd heard about her had made her sound eccentric, he could see that the woman was sharp. There was intelligence and humor in her penetrating gaze also. He doubted anyone could put much over on her.

"Thank you, but Virginia can pour," Pepper said.

"You have a beautiful place here, Mrs. Winchester. Let me know if you need anything else."

"Thank you." She hadn't taken her eyes off him since he'd come into the room. Did she know he wasn't who he was pretending to be?

"That will be all," Virginia snapped between bites of cookie. "I'm so hungry even Enid's horrible cookies taste good."

He saw Pepper's jaw tense in irritation. He smiled at Pepper and gave a slight bow before leaving the room.

"Where did Enid find *him?*" he heard Virginia say loud enough he couldn't help but hear—even if he hadn't stopped just outside the door.

"Sometimes, Virginia," Pepper said with obvious frustration.

"I don't mean to be irritable, Mother. It's my low blood sugar and Enid's horrible cooking and this weather. I need to get out of here for a while. I think I'll go into town."

TD heard her start toward the door. He ducked into the alcove until she passed, then hurried back to the kitchen. If one of the people in that room had called him, it wasn't because they knew him—or knew what he looked like. Nobody had reacted as if they recognized him.

The only person who seemed the least bit interested in him had been Pepper Winchester.

"WELL?" ENID DEMANDED when TD returned to the kitchen.

"Nothing to report," he said and went to work.

Enid had a big pot of what appeared to be vegetable soup cooking on the stovetop. When he finished unloading the groceries in the pantry, he noticed she had just measured flour into a large bowl.

"What's next?" he asked. She looked surprised that he was finished and he realized he might be out of a job too quickly if he wasn't careful. "What are you making?"

"Pies. Going to take at least four the way Virginia eats."

"What kind of pies?"

"They like apple, but I hate doing all that peeling."

"I don't mind. If it's okay with you," he added.

"Might as well earn your money," she said.

He wondered idly how much he was making as he found the apples and set to work peeling them—and encouraging Enid to talk.

"This is an awful lot of work for one woman," he said. "Am I your only help?"

"Pepper wanted to hire a cook from town," the old woman said. "She'd just love to put me out to pasture. Well, I'm not about to make it easy on her. I told her I'd take some help, but that was it and only until the wedding is over. I figure most of them will clear out by then."

"Those were her sons I just saw?"

"Brand and Worth. Worth is just here for the money. He's hoping his mother drops dead so he can get his share of the Winchester fortune." Enid laughed. "I wouldn't count on that if I were him. Brand, he's the younger one, he can't wait to get out of here. At least the grandsons who are moving up here are building their own places on the ranch far enough away I won't have to deal with them."

"How many grandsons are there?" he asked.

"Legitimate ones? Depends on who's counting. Four, I guess. Not to mention the granddaughter who's the sheriff."

"Pepper's granddaughter is the sheriff?"

Enid shot him a look. "McCall. She's the one getting married. Didn't they tell you anything when you applied for this job?"

"Not really." He watched her halfheartedly start to make the pie crusts. "You know my mother used to win blue ribbons at the county fair with her pie crust. She taught me her secret."

The phone rang.

He snatched up the phone before Enid could dust the flour from her hands and answer it. "Winchester Ranch."

The woman on the other end of the line was apologizing profusely because she'd just learned that the person she'd sent out to help at the ranch had gotten lost, then gotten stuck and was now waiting for a wrecker to get her out of the ditch.

"I know it's late but do you want me to send someone else?" the woman from the employment agency asked.

"No. Not necessary. It's quite all right."

"Then you don't need anyone?" She sounded relieved and he wondered if it was difficult to get someone to come out here to work. The locals would have heard all the horror stories about the Winchesters. Not to mention Enid.

"No, it's no problem." He hung up and saw Enid watching him with narrowed eyes. "Wrong number."

She didn't say anything for a moment, then, "I'll let you finish the pie crusts, if you're sure you know how. But I'll be watching you," she warned as she dusted flour from her hands onto her apron.

She wasn't the only one watching him, TD thought, as he sensed someone in the kitchen doorway and turned to see Pepper Winchester. She'd brought the tray back. He quickly took it from her and she left. But he wondered how much she'd heard. Too much, he thought, which could explain the suspicious look she'd given him.

"Now what?" TD asked later after the pies were baked and he'd helped serve an early lunch of soup and bread. Virginia, good to her word, had gone into town. The tension during the meal between Pepper and her two sons had been thick enough to cut with a hatchet.

It was hours before supper. Enid had said they were having steaks and he could grill them. She said she would put in the potatoes to bake and could make a salad while he did the steaks.

"I'm going to take a nap and get off my poor old feet," she said. "You're free to do whatever you want."

"I see you have horses."

"Hardly anyone rides them anymore," she said. "Help yourself. Just don't go too far. And don't be late to help with supper."

LIZZY CHANGED FOR LUNCH, dreading what she knew was going to be a tense meal. She was no fool. She knew that Janie didn't want her here. Anne, either, for that matter. Something was going on between the sisters.

It made her sad to think how close she and Anne had been as girls and how they had drifted apart. She blamed herself. She'd been so lost after her father's death and the ranch had been a painful reminder of that loss.

Later, after she'd gone to work for Roger Collins, she'd been so involved in her work that the few times she could get away, Anne had been busy.

Lizzy tried to put it out of her mind. She just needed to stay here until she could complete her assignment.

Lunch was as miserable as she'd anticipated. Both McCormick sisters seemed to be in a bad mood and said hardly a word.

"I think I'll take another ride after lunch, if that's all right," Lizzy said when it was finally over.

"You really don't have to ask every time," Anne snapped. "Please, just make yourself at home."

"Yes, you're more like family than a guest," Janie had said, shooting her sister a look of defiance.

Lizzy couldn't wait to get away from the pair. She took the satellite phone to make the call to her boss once she had ridden far enough away from the ranch. Stopping on a hill out of sight of the house, she made the call.

"Agent Calder reporting in," she said when Roger Collins answered.

"You made it to Montana without any trouble?"

"Yes, sir. We both did."

"TD is there?"

"He's apparently staying at the Winchester Ranch."

"How did he manage that?"

She had no idea and said as much.

"If there is any way you can make contact, do. Just be careful. TD Waters will be suspicious of anyone who tries to get close to him right now. Keep me posted."

Liz disconnected, thinking about the man she'd seen behind the wheel of the pickup—and the photograph of the boy. She realized she hadn't mentioned that she'd found the photograph among Waters's things. Or that the name on the back of the photograph was a different one, although the boy in the snapshot was clearly Waters.

She told herself the framed photograph was irrelevant. Her boss was more interested in what weapons he'd brought, where he was staying and what he was doing.

Why would Roger Collins care about some old photograph of Waters?

Lizzy was glad she hadn't mentioned it as she put away the phone and considered how to get closer to Waters.

The one thing she wouldn't let herself speculate on for long was why he'd gone rogue, and ultimately what she would be ordered to do to stop him if necessary. Best not to know too much, Agent Director Collins had always told her.

"Just do your job. No questions asked." He had smiled at her kindly. "One of these days you'll be tested. Don't let me down, Elizabeth."

She feared that day had come.

"McCALL, MAYBE YOU should consider hiring some security for the wedding. I'm serious," Luke said. They lay in the small double bed in his travel trailer after sneaking away for an impromptu lunch and lovemaking. Through the window, she could see the beautiful house he'd built for them. Luke had promised it would be finished and furnished by the time they returned home from their honeymoon. He'd also made her promise she wouldn't peek until then.

McCall looked over at her handsome fiancé. "This is about the McCormicks?"

"You said you picked up bad vibes from them."

She realized she shouldn't have shared that with him. They were both in law enforcement, but Luke was also a man. He worried about her.

"Don't you think my family is more dangerous than the McCormick sisters ever could be?" she asked, only half joking, as she lay back and stared up at the ceiling.

"I was thinking more of the bad blood between the two families," he said, still way too serious. "This will be the first time that all of the Winchesters are together in one place."

"The thought makes me nauseous. Maybe security isn't such a bad idea. We'll need someone to keep my mother and grandmother from killing each other. If I know my mother, she'll head straight for the bar at the reception. All Pepper has to do is look at her cross-eyed and all hell will break out."

Luke sighed, his expression impatient. "Not to mention," he continued as if she hadn't spoken, "the fact that your grandmother still believes that someone in the family was in on your father's murder."

As if she had forgotten. Her grandmother wasn't the only one who still believed that. The problem was that her father was dead and nothing could bring him back. Add to that she didn't like investigating her own family—the family she'd only recently even been accepted into.

But she was the sheriff and she had suspected that Sandy Sheridan had some reason for committing the murder within sight of the Winchester Ranch. Sandy had wanted someone to see it.

"Maybe the guilty family member is already dead," she said halfheartedly. "You know my uncle Angus drank himself to death. He wouldn't be the first person to drink because of guilt."

"Maybe." Luke sounded as doubtful as she felt. Everything she'd heard about Angus Winchester went against his being involved. "Now to find out that the McCormick girls were there that day and might have seen something. Everyone in the county knows that they blame Pepper for their mother going to prison."

"And everyone knows that is just crazy," she said as she leaned toward her fiancé and gave him a kiss. "But I do know what you're saying. There could be trouble at the wedding."

McCall had known that from the get-go. She needed to defuse at least some of it if possible before the wedding. She didn't tell him that she'd been investigating Pepper's three surviving offspring. The problem was that the wedding was looming and she still didn't have any evidence against any of them.

Worth Winchester had started a Western rope manufacturing business after he'd left the ranch and had done well. Brand had worked at a series of ranches and finally settled down to manage one in Wyoming. Virginia was the only one who didn't seem to have any visible means of support. From what McCall had been able to discover, she had gotten by through the largesse of a series of men.

If one of her father's siblings had been a coconspirator in Trace Winchester's murder, they'd keep that secret well.

"I don't like that look in your eye," Luke said. "I just want you to be careful. Think about security at the wedding. You never know what other skeletons could come clattering out of a closet."

McCall nodded to her fiancé although she thought it would be a relief to not have any more secrets. Her fear was that they might never learn if there had been a coconspirator in her father's murder—or who it was.

She couldn't help but worry what that would do to her grandmother. Pepper Winchester was bound and determined to learn the truth or die trying.

LIZZY LET HER HORSE RUN. The afternoon was sunny and bright, the snow ablaze with sparkling ice crystals. The air, while cool, felt wonderful. She felt alive on horseback and for a few minutes she almost forgot where she was going—or why.

That was until she saw the lone rider headed toward her.

TD Waters.

She pulled up short, realizing she must be on Winchester Ranch land. Collins had warned her not to make him suspicious. She thought it might be too late for that. Taking in her surroundings, she was more than aware of how alone the two of them were out here—miles from either ranch house. She doubted anyone would hear a gunshot, let alone a scream—if there was even a chance that he suspected she was an agent after him.

Her horse danced under her as if sensing her sudden anxiety. The mare was ready to run again. All Lizzy had to do was give her free rein.

The rider was coming fast. Tall and dark and dangerous. She could feel the weapon in the shoulder holster beneath her flannel-lined jean jacket, but she knew she would never be able to get to her gun in time if she needed it.

But unless her cover was blown or she blew it now, she wouldn't need to use her weapon. She reminded herself that if she were just meeting TD Waters, she wouldn't know how dangerous he was. If she just played it cool…

The problem was, she thought as he barreled toward her, this was the second time he'd seen her on the Winchester Ranch. That alone could be cause for suspicion—especially if he thought she was going out of her way to run into him.

Making the split-second decision, Lizzy spurred her horse and took off back the way she'd come. The mare was fast and she was an excellent rider.

She hadn't expected him to chase her—especially after she crossed the dry creek bed that marked the boundary to McCormick land. Both ranches were too large to fence and this part was only accessible by foot or horseback.

Lizzy knew she could outrun him on a horse. Riding like the wind, she let herself glance back, shocked to realize he was gaining on her. Nowhere in his dossier had it said he could ride. But this man was obviously as at home on a horse as she was—and he rode like her, as if he couldn't go fast enough.

Her hat suddenly blew off, sailing back on the wind.

She turned around in the saddle, but didn't slow. If she went back for the hat, for sure he'd think she'd dropped it on purpose.

To her amazement, he didn't slow as he

rode toward her hat, leaned down from his saddle as if he was riding in a Wild West show and scooped up it up from the snow. Was he crazy?

No, he was TD Waters, and she'd heard enough stories about him to know how capable the man was—as well as how unrelenting.

Lizzy realized she couldn't keep going or they would reach the McCormick house. The last thing she wanted was for Janie and Anne to know about Waters.

She also knew better than to play coy with the man—even if she was the type who could pull off coy. Along with the stories of Waters's exploits in the field, she'd also heard about his exploits when it came to women.

She could almost feel his horse breathing down her neck. Now or never, she thought, since it was clear he wasn't going to give up. She reined in her horse.

It was time she and TD Waters finally met.

Chapter Five

TD reined in his horse as the woman came to a stop. He saw her through the steam coming off their horses. If anything, his first glimpse of her on the road this morning had been flawed.

She was more than a little striking with her flaming auburn hair, her full mouth and that angelic face. One look into those wide, pale gray eyes and he lost his breath.

"If you're thinking of having me arrested for trespassing on Winchester land, I should tell you that you're now on the McCormick Ranch and they tend to shoot first and ask questions later," she said haughtily as their horses danced around each other as if sizing the other up—just as their riders were doing.

TD couldn't help but laugh. Her cheeks were flamed from the heat of the race across the open country and her apparent anger. Her wild mane of red hair floated around her shoulders, as wild as the look in those gray eyes of hers.

"You dropped your hat," he said and held it out to her.

She snatched it from his fingers and settled it on her head, her chin coming up in open defiance. "You could have gotten us both killed riding like that."

He smiled. "I could say the same of you."

"What do you want?" she demanded.

"I think you know."

She leveled those eyes at him. Was that a warning? Or a dare?

"Can we quit pretending now that you don't know who I am?" He caught her off guard and for a moment, he saw something else in those beautiful, thickly lashed eyes of hers. Uncertainty.

"I've never met you before in my life. I would have remembered someone as…overly aggressive as you are."

Overly aggressive? He laughed again. "You've apparently already forgotten about this morning on the road when you and your horse practically took out my pickup with me in it."

"Oh, was that you?"

As if she didn't know. He had to admire her ease at lying, and right to his face. She looked so damned innocent another man might have believed her. But why would she lie?

"When I saw you, you know what I said to myself?" he asked.

"I can hardly imagine."

He cocked his head at her. "I said I had to find that woman and give her a piece of my mind."

"You're sure you have that much to spare?"

He shook his head but couldn't help grinning. Didn't she realize she was no match for him? "Do you always ride like that?"

"Yes." Again that defiant upward tilt of the chin and that steely-eyed look that radiated both warning and challenge.

He studied her for a moment. Nothing could convince him, not even that angelic face or those sweet lies on her lips, that she hadn't recognized him earlier this morning. But he could see he wasn't getting anywhere with her. The timing felt wrong. Or maybe he just wanted an excuse to see her again.

Her horse moved restlessly under her, but the mare wasn't half as restless as the rider was to get away from him, and it was no act just for his benefit.

"I like the way you ride," he said.

A small smile curved her lips. "I could say the same of you."

"So, where are you from?" he asked glancing around and seeing nothing but wild open country.

"From?"

"You must live around here somewhere."

"The McCormick Ranch over that hill," she said.

"So you're a McCormick."

She shook her head. "A friend of the family. Are you a Winchester?"

"No, I'm just working there." He held out his hand, moving his horse closer to hers. "Name's TD Waters." He waited for her reaction as she took his hand. None at the name, but he felt her wince at his touch—just as he'd seen her surprise when he'd said he was working at the ranch.

As cool as the woman was pretending to be, she was jumpy as hell. Understandable, he assumed, given that a stranger had just chased her down on horseback. But he wasn't a stranger, was he?

"Lizzy Calder." She pulled back her hand the moment he released it.

"Lizzy? Short for Elizabeth, right?"

"It was my mother's name." She seemed to bite her tongue as if she hadn't wanted to get that personal with him. "I really should be getting back before my hosts come looking for me."

"A little late for that," he said and motioned behind her.

She turned and stiffened and he knew she'd seen what he had. A lone rider was headed in their direction. It was her reaction that surprised him. Lizzy Calder looked scared.

ANNE? WHAT WAS SHE doing riding this way? Lizzy'd had the feeling that neither Anne or Janie rode anymore.

She swore under her breath and turned, not sure how she was going to handle this. But to her surprise, TD Waters was just dropping over a rise out of sight in the distance.

"Lizzy?" Anne said as she rode up. Her gaze was on the horizon where Waters had just disappeared. "Who was that? One of the Winchesters?"

"No," she said resenting the question but feeling compelled to answer since she was a guest on the ranch. "It was someone who works for them." She'd been surprised when he said he was working there. Working as a rogue agent on some undercover assignment? What else could he be doing there?

"What was he doing on my land?" Anne demanded. She sounded angry and Lizzy again felt the bitterness in her old friend. What had happened to her over the years that had made her this way? Anne used to be so easygoing, so fun-loving and sweet. Now she was more like her sister.

You mean land you're in the process of selling, Lizzy wanted to say, but of course didn't. "It's my fault. I rode too far, ended up on the Winchester Ranch." She wasn't sure how long Anne had been watching them. Had she seen Waters chase her in this direction?

"Was he threatening you?" Anne demanded, already getting her hackles up, even though Waters merely worked for the Winchesters.

"No, he was just curious. He hadn't seen another rider. I think he was lonesome."

Her friend raised a brow. "Hadn't seen a woman who looks like you, you mean."

Lizzy tried to smile. She'd never been comfortable with her looks. Her hair was too red, her eyes, like her skin, too pale. She managed to keep her freckles hidden most of the time—unless she got out in the sun. Like now. Her cheeks would be covered with them if her face wasn't flaming with the heated memory of the intense way TD Waters had been looking at her.

He'd been so determined that she'd recognized him. And, of course, she had. It frightened her that he could read her so easily. Even in a split second. She wondered what else she had given away during their brief first meeting.

"Well, if this hired hand wants to see you, he'll have to call," Anne said. "I don't like anyone from the Winchester Ranch on my land."

"Are you going for a ride?" she asked Anne, afraid she might try to go after Waters. But her friend shook her head.

"Just checking on you. You'd been gone for a while. I was getting worried. There's talk of a storm coming in."

Lizzy said nothing. Her heart was still pumping from her wild horseback race across the snowy landscape with a rogue agent after her—not to mention coming face-to-face with him. Her pulse still throbbed just beneath her heated skin. She hadn't been prepared for the impact the man made in the flesh.

She'd only glimpsed his intensity the first time she'd seen him. Sitting astride a horse next to him, she'd felt the full power behind the man she'd heard so much about. No wonder he had a way with women. She'd looked into his bottomless ebony gaze, a shiver coursing through her that still chilled her. Her every instinct told her that this was a man you didn't want to mess with.

What if even Roger Collins didn't realize how dangerous Waters was?

They rode back to the ranch together, Anne insisting she was tired and going to bed early. Janie had gone into town and they'd let the hired help go for the holidays, so Lizzy would have to fend for herself in the kitchen this evening.

Lizzy couldn't have been more thankful. She couldn't bear another meal with the two sisters. She wondered idly why Janie had gone into town. Was it possible she was seeing someone? Neither sister had married. In fact, Lizzy wasn't even aware if either of them had boyfriends. It did make her wonder, though, if they'd both been soured on marriage because of their mother.

Lizzy went straight to her room after putting her horse and Anne's away. Once there though, she found herself pacing, too keyed up to sit still. She tried to shove thoughts of TD Waters away, but the man was persistent—both in and out of her thoughts.

What she needed was a little something to snack on and maybe a nice cold beer. Tiptoeing down the stairs, she started for the kitchen, when she caught another glimpse of the living room and that awful piece of modern artwork where the old photographs had been.

Maybe she would go down to the basement first and see if she could find photographs of her father. Otherwise, she suspected they would get tossed out, especially with the sisters selling the ranch.

Opening the basement door, she reached in and turned on the light before treading down the stairs. The basement had never been finished and had ended up being used for storage. She saw boxes of Christmas ornaments and realized with a start that she wasn't the only one ignoring the holiday.

She hadn't even noticed that Anne and Janie hadn't put up a tree and apparently had no plans to. That seemed sad, even though Lizzy herself doubted she would be home in time for Christmas—let alone have a tree this year.

Past the ornaments, she found the framed photographs and, pulling up an old rocker, sat down and began to go through them even though the light was almost too dim. She didn't dare take them all upstairs to the living room and no way was she toting them all the way up to her room to go through them.

There were so many more than she'd remembered. She realized that if she had her choice, she wouldn't get rid of any of them. These were records of the ranch's history.

She heard a thud. It sounded as if it had come from the top of the stairs. Maybe Anne had come down for some reason. Or Janie had returned. She listened, feeling a little spooked after her run-ins with Waters, then Anne.

When she didn't hear anything, she quickly sorted through the photographs, taking any showing her or her father.

Taking the tall stack of framed photographs, she started back upstairs and stumbled, almost falling as the lights suddenly went out.

"Hey!" she called from the pitch blackness. "Hey! I'm down here!"

No answer, but she heard someone close the door with a slight click.

Carefully she set the stack of framed photos down on a step, then felt her way up to the top of the stairs and turned on the light, her heart pounding.

She'd never liked the dark, hadn't even as a child although she couldn't remember when she'd first realized how terrified she was of total darkness.

Going back down the stairs, she picked up the stack of photos and was almost to the top again when she heard the door open again.

Janie was framed against the faint light. "Oh, is someone down there?"

She knew perfectly well someone was down there. Lizzy looked into Janie's face, saw the smirk, felt the hard gaze, but said nothing as she climbed the rest of the way up from the basement.

"What were you doing down there?" Janie asked, sounding not particularly interested.

"Anne said I could have any photographs I wanted."

"I guess she told you then that we're selling the ranch."

"What will you do?" She knew that neither Janie or Anne had started their careers. Both had attended college, but as far as she knew neither had ever worked.

Hunt had made his fortune years ago. The ranch must have made money, as well. Someone had definitely been supporting the two sisters.

"You mean like work?" Janie quirked a brow, that smirk back on her lips. "I'm not too worried about that. I've managed thus far and the ranch should bring a pretty good price. Too bad I have to split it with my sister."

Lizzy felt cold inside at Janie's words, and angry. "Since you obviously don't care what happens to the ranch and just want the money,

I would think the Winchesters would be interested in buying it," she said, then chastised herself for stooping to the other woman's level.

To her surprise Janie laughed. "The Winchesters will never have this land. I promise you that. If I have my way, there won't be any Winchesters around to buy it. That goes for anyone else who gets in my way."

With that she turned and disappeared back up the stairs, leaving Lizzy with the unmistakable feeling that TD Waters wasn't the only dangerous person she had to worry about.

WHEN TD RETURNED FROM his ride, he quickly showered, changed and hurried over to the kitchen. He'd been gone longer than he'd planned.

Enid gave him a sour look, but no more sour than usual. "Did you get lost? You were gone long enough."

He decided to see how much information about the McCormicks and Lizzy Calder he could get out of Enid, since she did love to gossip. "I rode south and stumbled across the McCormick ranch," he said as if just making conversation.

"Surprised you didn't get shot. If Joanna

McCormick wasn't in prison you would have been."

"I take it she didn't like the Winchesters?"

Enid huffed. "Not after Pepper tried to steal her husband. Bad blood between the families." She added conspiratorially, "Started over an affair."

"So this war between the Winchesters and the McCormicks began with an affair?"

"And some affair it was," Enid said warming to the subject. "Hunt McCormick asked Pepper to run away with him."

Pepper and Hunt McCormick? "But she didn't."

Enid shook her head. "She had her reasons." The old woman seemed to close up again. "I think Hunt McCormick was the true love of her life."

"Is he still alive?"

She nodded. "Pepper hasn't seen him for twenty-seven years. As far as I know, he's still married to Joanna. I heard she wouldn't give him a divorce, but they haven't lived together for years." He listened as she told how Joanna McCormick had ended up in prison for murder.

"There seems to be a lot of violence out here in the West," he said.

"You have no idea," Enid said. "No idea at all."

"I guess I was lucky the owner is in prison and the woman I ran across didn't try to shoot me."

"If she was a McCormick, you damned sure were lucky," Enid said. "That bad blood has spilled over onto the young ones. I wouldn't turn my back on either of them." She mugged a face. "They're both spoiled to high heaven. Anne isn't so bad, but her younger sister, Janie, was spawned by the devil." Enid crossed herself.

"Fortunately neither were McCormicks, I guess. The woman I ran across said her name was Lizzy Calder. Even heard of her?"

Enid frowned. "Calder. A Will Calder used to be the ranch manager over there, but he's been dead for some time. Wait, he had a daughter. A pretty little redheaded girl." Now beautiful, he thought. "I think she was friends with Anne McCormick. She over there, too?"

"Apparently."

"How'd you meet her?"

"She was out riding."

"Probably riding on Winchester land. All three of those girls always used to sneak over here. Thought nobody knew. Well, I knew all right. Come over here flirting with Pepper's grandsons. If she'd have caught them…" Enid wagged her head as if she didn't even want to imagine what would have happened.

"Why would Pepper have anything against the girls if she was the one who had the affair with this Joanna McCormick's husband?" he had to ask.

"It goes back a lot further than that." Enid clamped her lips together as if that was all she could say.

A secret, he thought.

"I'm going to give you some good advice. Stay clear of the McCormicks and that Calder woman, just do your job and don't ask any questions. And don't go mentioning this to any of the family," Enid said as she thrust a huge bowl of salad at him. "Virginia's probably starving. Take this out, then you'd better get on the steaks pronto."

Taking the salad, he stepped through the door into the dining room and saw that the family was gathered around the long table.

Virginia made a point of glancing at her watch before picking up her wineglass. She started to take a drink, but seemed to change her mind.

He served the salad, taking note of the Winchesters sitting around the table. Pepper sat at the head of the table, her son Brand on her right, her daughter, Virginia, on her left and Worth sitting as if on his own next to his brother. The rest of the chairs were empty.

It was easy to tell the brothers apart. From what Enid had said, he found himself thinking of Worth as the big, bitter one. Brand was the handsome one, the only decent one of the bunch, according to Enid. Virginia was simply, in Enid's terms, the bitch.

Just as he had finished serving the salad, a young woman appeared in the doorway, apologizing for being late. Even if she hadn't been wearing her sheriff's uniform, he would have known she had to be Pepper's granddaughter. They looked that much alike.

Sheriff McCall Winchester took a place at the table. He felt her gaze as he served her salad. Her interest in him made him a little nervous as he quickly filled her bowl and excused himself.

Back in the kitchen, he put down the bowl.

"They ate all of it?"

"The sheriff just arrived. I served her the last of it."

She studied him suspiciously. "The sheriff a problem for you?"

"Why would it be?"

"You tell me," she persisted. "I saw the way you looked as you hightailed it back in here. You wanted for something?"

He laughed. "The law is definitely not looking for me." But he knew there were others who definitely were. In fact, he was beginning to wonder what was taking them so long.

Chapter Six

Lizzy showered and changed, her stomach growling. She decided to sneak downstairs and see what she could find to eat. After her run-in with Janie, she'd lost her appetite and she'd felt dirty after rummaging in the basement for the photographs.

But now she was hungry and it was too early to turn in. As she started down the stairs, she heard an odd sound. The living room was dark, only faint light bled through the sheer curtains at the windows from the snowy landscape outside.

At the bottom of the stairs, she finally realized what she was hearing. In a corner of the living room she could make out a figure curled in one of the wicker chairs, crying.

"Anne?" She moved to her friend and put an arm around her. "Oh, Anne."

"Don't pretend you're my friend," Anne

snapped, shrugging off Lizzy's arm. "Where were you when my life fell apart?"

Probably in some foreign country working undercover. "I didn't know—"

"Exactly, you didn't know. Your mother and father adored each other. That's all I ever heard growing up. Everyone could see that it ripped your dad's heart out when your mother died."

Was she supposed to apologize because her parents loved each other?

"How do you think that made my mother feel?" Anne demanded, her face flushed with her fury. "You think my mother ran my father off?" She let out a hard laugh. "He left her."

"I'm so sorry," Lizzy said, pulling up a chair next to Anne.

"Hunt was even worse. He didn't just have an affair with Pepper Winchester. He was in love with her, had been since he was seventeen, mother told me. Apparently he'd come to Montana looking for Pepper."

"So how did he end up married to your mother?" Lizzy asked.

Anne shot her a look. "You think she tricked him into marrying her?"

She wouldn't have put it past Joanna, especially if she'd known that Hunt was in love with Pepper Winchester. Lizzy had a feeling that the problems between the two families went way back.

"Supposedly Hunt didn't know Pepper had married Call Winchester and was only a ranch away when he married my mother," Anne said. "He told my mother that Pepper was the love of his life. I think he was planning to have both this ranch and Pepper. Now do you understand?"

Lizzy felt her heart go out to Hunt—and Joanna. She tried to find something to say in the silence that stretched out between them. Something that wouldn't destroy their relationship.

Unfortunately, she'd seen the way Joanna had treated Hunt before they'd separated for good. She had undermined him, embarrassed him, embarrassed them all by being so mean and vindictive.

"I guess I wonder, knowing that, why didn't your mother just let him go? Anne, she was the one who wouldn't give him a divorce. Why hold on to a man who doesn't want you?"

Anne started to argue, but slumped back into the chair. "I don't know why."

"She didn't want him to be with Pepper," Lizzy said quietly.

Her friend looked up, anger flashed in her eyes but quickly died. "I don't like thinking of her being that hateful. I know she was cold and hard to get close to…"

"Hunt was always a good father to you girls," Lizzy said. "He wasn't a mean man. Your mother was hurt. That's understandable. But Anne, all that happened so long ago. It's time to let go of it. All these hateful feelings will only eat you up inside. Your mother could have found happiness with someone else, but she preferred to punish Hunt. Don't let the past ruin your future."

Tears welled in Anne's eyes. "I know you're right, but…"

Lizzy reached for her. Anne made a half-hearted attempt to push her away, then crumbled in her arms.

"I'm just so confused," Anne cried. "I don't want to sell the ranch but Janie does and I just feel too tired and depressed to fight her."

She rubbed her friend's back and tried to soothe her as Anne began to cry again. "Maybe if you give it more time…"

"What's going on?"

Lizzy looked back to see Janie at the edge of the room. Suddenly the room was flooded with light as Janie snapped on the lights.

Anne pulled away, hurriedly drying her eyes as she got to her feet. "I'm just overly tired. I'll see you in the morning."

"Stay out of our business," Janie said after Anne's bedroom door closed upstairs. "Don't go putting ideas in Anne's head." She gave Lizzy a hard glare before turning away without another word.

"IT'S PRETTY TENSE IN THERE," TD whispered to Enid as the dining-room door closed behind him.

Enid gave him a knowing look from the kitchen table, where she was sitting with her feet up. "I told you I wouldn't be surprised if there was a murder before this was over."

"Don't they want the sheriff to marry this game-warden fiancé of hers?" He'd picked up a lot of information about this family thanks to Enid. Too bad he wasn't any closer to finding out who had called him from here.

"She can marry anyone she wants and her grandmother would be pleased as punch." Enid shook her head. "It isn't about the wedding."

"I don't understand then, but you aren't serious about someone getting murdered," TD said.

She let out a bark of a laugh. "You saw that in there. The old gal is up to her tricks."

"I saw Mrs. Winchester watching all of them."

"She's watching them all right. She believes one of them was in on the murder of her youngest son, Trace, twenty-seven years ago. Killed right over there on that ridge," Enid said, pointing out the window.

He saw the ridge in the distance. A deep ravine separated the ranch from the murder site. "Why would one of his own siblings—"

"Because he was the youngest, the favorite. Pepper loved him the best and the others hated him and her for it. Still do."

"Do you think she's right? That one of them was in on it?"

"I wouldn't be the least bit surprised and when Pepper figures out which one it was…." She let the rest of her thought hang in the air.

What was Pepper capable of doing if and when she found out? He glanced toward the dining room and wondered if it wasn't more likely that one of them would do in their mother. He'd seen the size of the ranch. There was money here, and where there was money, there was powerful motive.

Same could be true, though, for getting rid of the favorite younger brother.

"What would make her think that one

of them was involved?" he asked out of curiosity.

"Pepper became suspicious after she found five party hats—and a small pair of binoculars—in a third-floor room that her husband used to punish the kids. He'd lock them in there. All except Trace. She wasn't having her youngest put in that room. Another reason the others hated him."

"Five party hats?"

"The day of the murder was Trace Winchester's birthday. Pepper was throwing him a big party. That's why the family was here—Brand's two boys, Cyrus and Cordell, and Jack, who turned out to be Angus Winchester's son with the nanny."

"But you said there were five—"

"Had to be those McCormick girls," Enid said with disgust. "I wonder if Pepper's figured it out. Oh, she is going to be hotter than a pistol when she does."

The McCormick girls. He glanced toward the window and the far ridge across the ravine where Enid said Trace Winchester had been murdered.

What a tangled web the Winchester family was turning out to be.

After he helped Enid finish up in the kitchen, he walked down to his cabin near the barn. The night was cold, but not as cold as he thought it should have been in this part of Montana so close to Christmas.

He slowed. Ahead, the horses moved restlessly in the corral. One whinnied and was answered by another at the dark edge of the corral.

TD told himself there wasn't anyone waiting on the dark side of the bunkhouse. Still, he stood listening. He knew it would be hard to start carrying a concealed weapon in the kitchen, but he also knew it wouldn't be long before Roger Collins sent someone to take care of him.

He didn't want to be unarmed when that happened. Like tonight.

The horses settled down, and all was quiet again. He took a moment to stare up at the magnificent canopy of stars sparkling in the deep blue of the night sky overhead. Wow, he'd forgotten how incredible a Montana night sky could be away from the lights of town.

"It's amazing, isn't it?" asked a voice from the deep shadows beside his cabin, startling him.

He'd been so sure his first instinct had been wrong. Fortunately, he recognized the voice at once and smiled to himself as he stepped over to the side of the building.

Lizzy stood in the deep shadows leaning against the log wall, clearly waiting for him. Even though she was in shadow, starlight reflected off the snow, and he could see that his first impression of her hadn't been exaggerated. The woman was a beauty, one of those women who turned a man's head.

TD knew she was the last thing he needed right now and yet he couldn't hide his pleasure at seeing her again. He noted that her horse was tied up behind the corral. That was why the horses had been restless just moments earlier. But somehow she had calmed them all down. She seemed to have that effect on horses, but just the opposite effect on him.

This woman stirred up something powerful in him. Few women had ever done that. None had intrigued him the way this one did.

"What a pleasant surprise," he said. "I wasn't sure when I would see you again." There had been no doubt in his mind, though, that he was going to see her again soon, and he suspected she knew that.

"I came to apologize. Earlier—"

"There's no need. You were just protecting me from being shot for trespassing. I appreciated your concern."

She smiled at that. "You also rescued my

hat." She touched the brim. "Since it's my favorite, thank you again."

TD knew she'd come over here for something other than to apologize or to thank him. "It was the least I could do. It isn't every day a woman takes you for the ride of your life."

She looked uneasy.

"Aren't you afraid you'll get caught over here?" he asked, glancing back toward the lodge. Lights blazed in the main windows but no sound moved on the night breeze.

"I've been sneaking over here since I was a girl."

He laughed softly. "You still like the thrill that you might get caught."

"You're on to me."

He eyed her, suspecting he was nowhere near understanding this woman. "Would you like to come in?" he asked, motioning toward the door of the cabin. "It's a bit austere but it's warm inside."

She shook her head as she pushed herself off the wall. "I need to get back, but thanks."

"You sure you'll be all right riding back alone? If you need company..."

She flashed him a grin. "I like riding alone. With the snow on the ground and the stars out, it's almost as bright as daylight."

He wanted to ask her why she'd really come

over as she untied her mount and swung up into the saddle. But whatever little game they were playing, he was more than happy to play along.

"Good night, Mr. Waters." She tipped her hat and rode off.

He watched her go, his smile fading. He felt a chill that could have been the night air or the uneasy feeling that settled in him as she disappeared over the rise. Whatever was bothering him, it was more than Lizzy Calder's unexpected visit.

He started to open his cabin door when he saw a dark figure standing under the overhang at the front of the main lodge. How long had Worth Winchester been there? His head was turned toward the horizon—the same one Lizzy Calder had just dropped over. Even from this distance, TD could see the anger in the man's stance before Worth stepped back inside the lodge.

Would he report what he'd seen to his mother?

This feud between the McCormicks and Winchesters was more than bad blood, TD thought as he slipped inside his dark cabin and closed the door against the December night.

It wasn't until he turned on a light that he saw the envelope that had been pushed under his door.

WHEN LIZZY RETURNED, it was late. The night had gotten colder, not that she'd noticed. Being around Waters had her plenty heated. She could feel her cheeks still flaming. It was the way he looked at her. She swore it was as if he could see her not just naked—but exposed clear to her soul.

She put her horse away and tried to put away thoughts of Waters with the mare. She was reminded of the late-night rides she and Anne used to go on and sneaking back into the house so they didn't get caught.

Fortunately, there was no one downstairs when she came into the house this time. Before her ride, she'd made herself a sandwich but had been too restless to eat it in the kitchen. She had wandered down to the barn, eating her sandwich and worrying about Anne.

She'd realized that what she should have been worrying about was her next move with rogue agent TD Waters. That was when she'd decided to pay him a little visit.

Surprising him had been a good idea, she thought now. He hadn't expected to see her. She liked that she'd put such a confident man a little off balance. She guessed it was something TD Waters wasn't used to.

She smiled to herself as she tiptoed upstairs and slipped into the guest room, remembering the way his dark eyes had shone when he saw her—and his even bigger surprise when she didn't take him up on his invitation to come inside his cabin.

With his reputation, she liked being the woman who'd turned him down. Not that she didn't understand how a woman could find herself under his spell. The man wasn't just drop-dead gorgeous; he had the powerful magnetism of a man who knew exactly who he was and what he wanted out of life. No woman alive could resist that—and TD Waters knew it.

As Lizzy turned on the light, she saw the stack of framed photographs sitting on the desk in her room. She hadn't really had a chance to go through them.

Now, still restless and needing to think of anything but her assignment and TD Waters, she moved to the desk and, turning on the light, began to go through the old photographs, slowly this time.

Tears welled in her eyes as she touched her father's face in one of the photographs. He looked so handsome, so happy. His Western hat was pushed back; he was smiling at the camera from atop of a large black horse.

Hunt was beside him on one side and another man sat to his left, both also on horseback.

Lizzy squinted at the photograph of the other man. He looked almost…familiar. She adjusted the lamp, dusting off the glass in the frame.

Her heart began to beat harder. For a moment she couldn't catch her breath. The man in the photograph next to her father… No, it couldn't be. He was much younger, had more hair, looked so different, and yet there was no doubt.

It was Roger Collins, the director of the agency.

How was that possible? Her father had known Collins?

Turning the frame over, she worked the photograph out. The date and the names of the people in the photo were written on the back.

There was no getting around it. Roger Collins had been on the ranch back when he was still an agent like herself. Roger Collins had known her father. She checked the date again. She'd been eleven that summer, too young to remember him since a lot of people came and went at the ranch, and she and Anne had been too busy to notice or care.

But Roger should have remembered her and her father.

Lizzy had to sit down. She was trembling all over. Wouldn't her boss have mentioned that he'd been to the McCormick Ranch, that he'd known her father, when he'd recruited her?

He'd recruited her after her father had died. Had her father known he was going to do that? Her father must have known what Roger Collins did for a living. Was it possible the two had planned her future?

Or had Collins purposely waited until her father was gone?

Lizzy shook off the rush of suspicions. She was jumping to conclusions based on nothing more than an old photograph. So what if the two had known each other? That didn't prove anything.

Still she couldn't help the unsettling feeling she got when she looked at the photo. She remembered one of the last times she and her dad had talked. It had been right before her college graduation. He'd offered to send her to Europe, said he'd even meet her over there.

But by then Roger had already recruited her.

Now, as she sat holding the photograph,

she knew it hadn't been a coincidence that she'd been given this particular assignment—Collins had known about her connection to the McCormick Ranch for years.

TD INSPECTED THE PLAIN white envelope before carefully opening it. He told himself it could be a note from Lizzy Calder—and the real reason she'd stopped by.

But it didn't look like a love letter.

It wasn't.

He read what was typed on the single sheet of paper:

I'm pleased to see you are as capable as I thought you were. You've made it to Montana. You should be rewarded for that so I'm going to give you a little something. Don't worry, I still want my money, but now that I've met you, I can see that you might need a little persuading. So here it is: Whitehorse Sewing Circle.

TD stared at the note, his mind racing. The person who'd called him had purposely led him to Montana and the Winchester Ranch and he'd come like a dog on a leash. He stared at the note. Was it possible Lizzy Calder had something to do with this?

Glancing around the cabin, he didn't see anything amiss. He knew he was being paranoid. Lizzy couldn't have been the one who called him from the Winchester Ranch. She didn't have access to a phone here on the ranch. At least he didn't think she did.

No, she'd just come over tonight to apologize. Or maybe she'd had more on her mind, but had chickened out at the last minute or was just toying with him.

He shook his head. She wasn't the type to chicken out. He'd seen the way she rode a horse. That woman wasn't afraid of anything. Nor did he get the feeling she'd been toying with him. When she wanted something, he suspected she went after it and didn't let anything get in her way.

The more likely suspect was Worth Winchester.

But TD couldn't shake the feeling that Lizzy had ridden over for more than an apology. He hoped to hell she wasn't involved. He liked her and it had been a long time since he'd really liked a woman he found that attractive. This one he didn't just want to get into bed. But that would definitely be a place to start, he thought, smiling to himself as he read the note again.

What the hell was the Whitehorse Sewing Circle? And what did that have to do with his past, if anything?

Someone was pulling his strings. TD couldn't wait to find out who and cut the cord permanently.

Chapter Seven

Lizzy woke early after a restless night. The first thing she saw was the photograph of her father and Roger Collins. She quickly got out of bed and buried it deep in one of her suitcases.

She didn't know what it meant—if anything. She hadn't talked to her boss since her call yesterday saying Waters was in Montana at the Winchester Ranch, but that hadn't come as a surprise to Roger Collins. He had told her he'd suspected that was where Waters was headed when he'd sent her to Montana.

He just hadn't told her why he'd suspected it or why Waters was on the ranch. She tried not to worry about either, but she couldn't help being even more curious about what had made Waters go rogue. He didn't seem like a man on the run. Far from it.

She thought about watching him come across the yard in the starlight last night, the cold December night exhilarating—just as sneaking over to see him had been. She remembered the way he'd pushed back his Western hat, the lazy way he'd leaned against the corner of the cabin as he'd looked at her with his dark, hooded eyes.

Lizzy felt a tremor at the memory. Her heart had taken off at a gallop with the sudden knowledge that he'd thought she'd come there last night to seduce him. It could have been a hot summer night the way her body had warmed under his black gaze. Had she gone inside the cabin with him, he would have been the one to seduce her.

She shook herself from the thought. Not that she would have fallen for it. But the point was, Waters definitely wasn't acting like a man running from his past or the agency. If he'd gone rogue, he certainly wasn't worried about anyone coming after him.

Unless he somehow knew Collins had sent her and wasn't in the least bit worried about her taking him in—or out, for that matter.

Lizzy headed for the shower, telling herself that TD Waters didn't know who he was dealing with. She definitely was not a woman who could easily be seduced. But as she stripped off her clothing and stepped under the spray, she felt her skin tingle at even the thought of being seduced by TD Waters.

Angry with herself, Lizzy showered quickly. Why was she feeling unsure about everything? It was that blasted photograph of Roger Collins. She just wished she could get the photograph of her boss on the McCormick Ranch astride a horse next to her father out her mind. It didn't mean anything. So why couldn't she free herself of the thought that nothing was as she once thought it?

She was letting the photo change her feelings about her boss—and her job. More to the point, this assignment. She was questioning everything. It was none of her business what Waters had come here for. He'd lulled her into thinking he was just this charming cowboy who was safe and innocent even though she knew better.

She reminded herself that she was a good agent on her way up. Roger Collins had done her a favor getting her in the agency. He was counting on her to come through.

So she'd do the job she'd been sent to do—no matter what Roger Collins asked her to do. No matter how much charm Waters turned on. No matter how many doubts she had about this assignment—or her boss.

After her shower, Lizzy felt a little better.

It was still early in the morning, too early. She wondered what she was doing up at this hour. She'd just finished dressing when she saw someone ride past outside. Stepping to the window, she watched Janie ride out, headed toward the northwest.

Her worry now turned into a hard knot of fear. Janie had never been an early riser. Nor had she ever liked to ride. Lizzy doubted that had changed.

So where was she going so early in the morning and on horseback?

Before she could talk herself out of it, Lizzy headed for the stables. She had a bad feeling and couldn't bear the thought of Anne being hurt any more than she had been already. As she watched Janie disappear over the hill, Lizzy knew where she was headed. The Winchester Ranch. The question was why?

TD HEARD SOMEONE OUTSIDE his cabin just before the sun came up. He stepped to the window, but it was too dark to see anything. Was it the person who'd left him the note? No. That person had gotten him to the ranch and was now feeding him clues. The first had been Winchester Ranch. The second was Whitehorse Sewing Circle. He still wondered what that was and what it could possibly have to do with him.

But what bothered him the most was if the person wanted fifty thousand, then why give him any clues at all?

He shook his head. Whatever. All he cared about was getting the answers, and since he had no intention of giving the person a dime…

Right now he needed to find out what was going on outside. Dressing quickly, he started out of the cabin as someone took off on a horse. He didn't get a good look, but his instincts told him to follow the rider. TD pulled on his holster and pistol and headed for the corral.

The rider crested the ridge in the semi-darkness of the coming dawn behind the Winchester lodge. The morning was cold as TD swung up into the saddle and rode in the direction he'd seen the early-morning rider heading. Fortunately, the rider was leaving tracks in the crusty snow and would be easy to trail.

Enid had said no one rode the horses anymore. And to leave this early, TD was betting something was up.

He slowed as he neared the top of the ridge where he'd last seen the rider. The sun rimmed the badlands to the east, showering the fallen snow in gold crystals. It was a blinding sight and he was awed by it. He hadn't realized that he'd missed Montana, missed all this wide open space, missed a simpler life. The last really did come as a surprise.

Rolling prairie stretched as far as the eye could see. It was deceiving, appearing perfectly flat when in fact the land was filled with narrow coulees and deep ravines chocked with stunted juniper and sage and jagged rock outcroppings.

What wild remote country. A person could get lost here and never be found, TD thought, afraid that was exactly what had happened this morning. There was no sign of the rider. Worse, there were no tracks up here on this rocky ridge where the snow had blown off.

He'd lost whomever he'd been following. Or had he? he thought as he heard the soft whinny of a horse in the distance.

LIZZY SADDLED UP AND rode out the way she'd seen Janie headed. The day was cold, the winter sun weak as it came up in a clear and cloudless sky.

Janie had too much of a head start for Lizzy to see her as she rode through the cold winter morning. As the sun rose, she followed the trail of fresh tracks Janie's horse had made in the snow. Lizzy's dad had taught her how to track when she was a girl. She'd learned the tracks of all the animals in the area and could easily tell the difference between a deer and an elk, a coyote and an antelope—or even the horses.

Janie seemed to be riding toward the back side of the ranch, circling through a more remote area. As Lizzy rode along, she kept her eye on the horizon, even though she didn't think Janie would be worried about being followed.

It was easy to lose herself in the beautiful winter day and the feel of the powerful horse beneath her. She loved this and realized how much she'd missed this kind of freedom.

It surprised her that Anne wasn't interested in the ranch or horseback riding anymore. Anne had loved it so much. She reminded herself that her memories of the ranch were completely different from Anne's and Janie's.

At the top of a hill, Lizzy stopped to scan the horizon. Still no sign of Janie but her horse's tracks led down a narrow ravine through a stand of junipers. Spurring her horse, she dropped down into the ravine.

She hadn't gone far when she spotted Janie's horse tied to a scrub pine a dozen yards ahead. Pulling up short, Lizzy slid from her horse next to a large juniper out of sight of Janie's horse. Tying her reins to a limb of the juniper, she crept closer, staying down behind an outcropping of rock.

Peering over the rock, she saw Janie with her back to her. She appeared to be waiting for something. For someone?

The thought was barely out before Lizzy saw a man approaching, leading a horse. He came from the direction of the ranch lodge. For just an instant, she thought it might be TD Waters and was relieved to see it wasn't.

This man was large, dark-headed and somber-faced.

"I told you I would contact you when I had the money," the man said, biting off each word. "Twenty-five thousand dollars is a lot of money to raise on such short notice."

Janie's laugh had a knife's edge to it. "But the alternative is so much worse, wouldn't you agree, Mr. Winchester?"

He shook his big head like an angry bull. "I don't like being blackmailed. You don't want to force me to do something you'll regret."

Janie laughed again. "It's you who is about to force me to do something you'll regret. What would happen if I went to your mother?"

He took a menacing step toward her but she stood her ground.

"Touch a hair on my head and the letter I've left in case of my death goes to your mother. We both know where that would leave you, now don't we?" Janie demanded angrily. "I want the money by tomorrow. No more excuses, Worth."

Worth Winchester?

Lizzy ducked down, but Janie didn't look in her direction as she stalked over to her horse. For an instant, she feared that Janie would ride back the way she'd come and see not only Lizzy—but also her horse.

Fortunately, Janie rode off toward the east and the rising sun.

Staying hidden, Lizzy didn't dare move as she heard Worth Winchester swing up into his saddle, the leather groaning under his weight. She listened to the jingle of his reins as the sound died off in the distance and started to turn to retrieve her own horse when she heard a faint, unmistakable sound behind her. It was then that she realized she'd made a mistake. She should have brought her gun.

LIZZY CALDER SWUNG around looking ready for a fight.

TD quickly held up both hands in surrender,

unable to keep from smiling. "Easy," he said, enjoying the spirit he saw in her.

She opened her mouth as if to say something but quickly closed it. He'd surprised her and now watched as she seemed to be trying to come up with an explanation for what she'd been doing other than the obvious.

"Don't like being caught spying?" he asked, not about to let her off easy.

"I wasn't spying."

He grinned. "Sure looked that way to me."

She brushed angrily at the snow she'd gotten on her jeans while hiding behind the rocks. "Which begs the question, what are you doing here? Spying on me? Or are you going to try to convince me you just happened along?"

"Nope. I'm just as guilty as you."

"I followed my friend because I was worried about her."

"As you should be, since apparently she's a blackmailer."

Lizzy seemed surprised that he'd also heard the conversation. "That doesn't explain why you were spying on *me*."

He grinned. "I was just enjoying the view. You have no idea how interesting it was."

She stopped brushing snow from the back of

her jeans as she realized he was talking about her derriere. "You should be ashamed."

"Really? 'Cause I'm not."

"You are incorrigible."

"I've been told that." He sobered. "Seriously, your friend is in trouble. Blackmail is a nasty business. It could get her hurt. So do you have any idea what that was about?"

"None." A lie. The woman just couldn't seem to help herself. She had no idea how easy she was to read. Like before when he'd seen recognition in those beautiful gray eyes and she'd denied it.

"Your friend's blackmailing Worth Winchester and you can't even imagine why?"

She squirmed under this gaze. "I might have my suspicions, but I'm sure you wouldn't be in the least bit interested."

"I might surprise you."

Her eyes narrowed. "What is it you said you do for the Winchesters?"

"I help cook."

She laughed. "Sure you do."

"I'm a hell of a cook, I'll have you know. If you'd ever had one of my pies, you'd be madly in love with me. Wouldn't be able to help yourself."

She actually blushed. He was even more intrigued with this woman. Not that he wasn't aware that she might not be quite as sweet and innocent as he'd first suspected.

"I really need to get back to the ranch before I'm missed."

"Hold on a second," he said. "What's your interest in Worth Winchester? Hell, what's your interest in all the Winchesters? And don't bother to lie. You aren't very good at it. Why else have you been sneaking over here for years?" He grinned. "And why sneak over here last night pretending you came to see me?"

"I did come to see you," she blurted, then clamped her lips shut as she straightened her shoulders, eyeing him. "You thought I had an ulterior motive when I came by to apologize to you?"

"It crossed my mind." Somewhere nearby a horse whinnied. His horse answered and he saw Lizzy's eyes widen a little.

"You followed Worth up here," she said.

"Curiosity."

"I guess you never heard what it did to the cat."

He laughed. Damn, but he liked this woman. "I think we should join forces."

"Is this about your pie-baking again?"

TD cocked his head at her, still smiling. "Something is going on with the Winchesters and the McCormicks. I think since we both have a stake in this, we should try to find out what it is."

"I'm sorry, what was your stake in this again?"

"I like these people," he said simply. "I don't want to see them hurt."

He could see she wasn't moved by that. Or she was doing a great job of hiding it. He figured he had nothing to lose by confiding in her, especially when he could use her help. Clearly the bad blood between the Winchesters and McCormicks was playing a part in all this.

"While I'm being honest with you...I wasn't always a cook's helper. I came here to find an extortionist," TD said.

She opened those gray eyes a little wider. "Why would someone want to extort money from you?"

He grinned. "Did I say this was about me?"

LIZZY HAD HAD ENOUGH of his games. She pushed off the rocks and headed for her horse. As she started past him, he caught her by the arm and turned her in to him. She felt just how strong he was even though his touch was gentle as he drew her to him.

She went like metal to a magnet, as if she had no choice, had never had a choice. He brushed his lips over hers, light as a snowflake, and she felt her lips part of their own accord. Then his mouth covered hers and she felt as if he had lifted her off her feet.

Then the kiss ended as quickly as it had begun. Her feet hit the ground again and she stumbled back, stunned that she'd actually not only let him kiss her, but that for a moment she had been kissing him back.

She looked into his dark eyes and felt him try to steal a little piece of her heart. And he would have, too, if he hadn't grinned just then, making her want to wipe it off his face.

"I've been wanting to do that since you and your horse almost totaled my pickup," he said. "Now that we got that over with, could we level with each other?"

The sun caught in his dark hair, making it shine like obsidian. His eyes shone just as brightly as he looked at her. She was reminded again of who this man was. Not just an agent, but a rogue agent, a very dangerous man. That kiss proved it.

"I told you what I was doing here," she said, reminded that he'd just told her she was a terrible liar. "I had a good reason to follow her.

Did you have as good a reason to follow one of your employers?"

He smiled at that. He had one of those smiles that threatened to melt something inside her. "All right, if that's the way you want to play it, I'll tell you what I think she has on Worth Winchester. She saw him from that third-floor room down there," he said motioning toward the lodge. "She looked across the deep ravine to that ridge."

She followed his gaze remembering what the sheriff had asked the sisters—about some binoculars and what the two of them had seen. Anne swore she hadn't seen anything. But Janie said she had seen something. Trace Winchester murdered?

"I've heard that Pepper Winchester suspects one of the family was a coconspirator in her youngest son's murder—and was on the ridge that day," he continued. "If I were a betting man, I'd put my money on Worth Winchester."

Lizzy'd had the same thought when she'd heard Janie threatening Worth. "So go to the sheriff."

"I think even up here in the Wild West they still require evidence," he said.

"So this extortionist brought you to Montana?" she asked. "Is it possible Janie has something on you? Or is it Worth Winchester who does?"

He laughed. "I told you what I suspected. Don't you owe me something in return?"

"I think the kiss makes us even," she said as she started past him again. She thought he might grab her again, but he didn't.

As she walked to her horse, she heard him chuckling behind her and knew he was looking at her behind. The man really was incorrigible, she thought as she touched her fingers to her lips.

BACK AT THE LODGE, TD found Enid in the kitchen and fell in beside her, picking up a spatula and seeing to the home fries she had going on the griddle.

"She eats like it might be her last meal," she complained as she pulled the eggs out of the refrigerator. "Virginia asked for an omelet. An *omelet.* She acts like she's staying at some fancy hotel."

"I can make the omelets," he said. "She say what kind she wants?"

If looks could kill, Enid's would have made him deader than a doornail.

He shrugged under the heat of it. "Just thought keeping them happy might prevent the murder."

Her face seemed to crack open as she laughed. "Can't make these people happy." But she added, "Ham-and-cheese omelet." She was already digging both out of the refrigerator.

He made the omelets on the griddle, moving the potatoes to a skillet on the back burner as she set about getting orange juice and glasses ready.

She was good and worked up and complained the whole time. He listened to her gripe about the family and gathered that she hadn't had anyone to complain to since her husband died a few months before.

He slid four perfect ham-and-cheese omelets onto a platter around a pile of home-fried potatoes and held them up for her approval.

She let out a snort, then picked up the tray with the orange juice and glasses and they headed for the dining room.

This morning, he noticed as he put down the food, only one person was missing, Worth. Was he just running late? Or was he skipping breakfast as he tried to figure out how to come up with twenty-five thousand dollars?

"Excuse me?" Pepper said to him.

TD looked up into Pepper Winchester's dark eyes and remembered Lizzy's visit last night and Worth seeing her. He now wondered if he'd been right about Worth tattling to his mother. He figured he was about to find out.

"Enid tells me you made the pies yesterday," the elderly matriarch said.

"Yes, ma'am."

"I just wanted to tell you that they were delicious."

"Thank you." He heard Enid make a rude sound nearby.

"I assume you also made the omelets this morning?"

"Yes, I've been trying to help Enid as much as possible. She's got enough on her hands as it is."

Pepper Winchester smiled, a light coming into her dark eyes. "That is very kind of you. You are the first help Enid has allowed me to hire for her. I'm glad the two of you are getting along so well."

"Enid's teaching me," TD said.

As Worth entered the dining room, TD took his leave, Enid trailing along behind him. The minute the door closed, Enid demanded, "Why didn't you take all the credit in there?"

"I just spoke the truth. This is way too much for one person to do." He smiled at her. "Can

I make you something for breakfast? Would you like an omelet?"

"Why not? I can be as snooty as that Virginia. Why not let someone wait on me for a change?"

"My thought exactly," he said as he made them both breakfast. "I saved us a couple pieces of apple pie if you're interested."

She smiled, a real honest-to-goodness smile, and took the slice of pie he offered her.

"Enid, I heard someone mention the Whitehorse Sewing Circle," he said as he sat down, watching her devour her omelet before he cut into his. "What's the deal with it?"

"A bunch of old women who make quilts for all the babies born around Old Town Whitehorse," she said.

What could that have to do with him? He didn't remember ever having a quilt. But maybe they kept track of births in the area.

"Why are you asking about them? You haven't knocked up your girlfriend, have you?"

He started to say he didn't have a girlfriend. So why did Lizzy Calder come to mind?

Before he could deny it, Enid said, "Is that really why you came to work out here? I knew you were too good to be true," she snapped, but she sounded relieved, as if she had suspected he had a lot worse to hide. "So you're looking to get rid of this kid."

He stared at her in shock. "Are you trying to tell me that this Whitehorse Sewing Circle does—"

"Under-the-radar adoptions. Don't act like you didn't know that."

He couldn't hide his relief. He'd been thinking something entirely different. Adoptions. Under-the-radar adoptions. If he really was adopted, then the adoption hadn't been legal. This was starting to make more sense.

"I'm just having trouble imaging a group called the Whitehorse Sewing Circle involved in—"

She laughed. "I know it's hard to believe a bunch of old-lady quilters are running an illegal adoption ring. That's probably how they've been able to get away with it for years. Remember, you didn't hear any of this from me."

"You have my word. Where would I find this sewing circle?"

PEPPER WINCHESTER SAT AT the head of the long wooden table and studied her sons and daughter as they finished their breakfast. It had been another uncomfortable meal. She wondered how many more of them she could stand.

Fortunately Christmas and the wedding were only two days away. Unfortunately she was no closer to finding out which of her wonderful children was a killer. Maybe the person at this table hadn't struck the blow that killed her son Trace, but he or she had still been part of it.

She looked around the table. *Which one of you helped get my precious Trace killed?* She'd thought that once she had them back at the ranch, she would just be able to look into their faces and see the truth.

How naive she'd been. Had she thought one of them would break down and confess? It was laughable now.

No, whoever it was intended to take their crime to the grave with him. Or her, she thought, eyeing her daughter before shifting her gaze to Brand, then Worth. Brand had always been the quiet, easygoing one. Still waters ran deep, she thought, though she couldn't imagine him doing such a thing.

Worth she could easily imagine getting involved in murdering his younger brother. Virginia...she definitely had it in her. Actually, all three of them did, she thought, remembering that they had her blood running through their veins. Her blood and Call Winchester's.

Against her better judgment, Pepper was considering giving Worth at least enough money that she didn't have to worry about him doing anything crazy and spoiling McCall's wedding. It went against the grain. She didn't like being blackmailed. Nor was it the first time. She thought of Enid.

Enid Hoagland had her over a barrel, so to speak. And for years Pepper had been thinking about putting the miserable wretch out of her misery.

As each of her offspring excused themselves and left, Pepper started to leave as well, but stopped when TD Waters came in to clear the table.

"I'm sorry," he said seeing her still sitting there. "I can come back."

"No," she said quickly. "I'd like a moment of your time." She looked past him to see that Enid had come into the dining room. "Alone, if you don't mind, Enid."

AS PEPPER MOTIONED FOR him to sit down, TD didn't like the feel of this, but pulled out a chair and joined her.

Enid scowled, shooting TD a suspicious

glance before leaving and letting the kitchen door slam.

In the quiet that followed, the matriarch merely studied him. "You're not from Whitehorse." It wasn't a question, but he answered anyway.

"No, ma'am."

"How is it you ended up in my kitchen?" she asked pointedly when he didn't elaborate.

He'd known this was probably coming. He'd seen her watching him closely, a little too closely. "I just kind of stumbled onto the job," he said truthfully.

"Are you a cook?"

"I like to cook."

Her eyes narrowed. "Is it just me or are you being purposely evasive?"

He scratched the back of his neck and considered telling her he'd come here to look for a blackmailer-extortionist.

"I'm a federal agent when I'm not cooking."

Her eyebrows shot up.

"I was wounded, had some time to kill and ended up in Montana."

"Wounded?"

"My last assignment didn't go like I thought it would," he said, the words like sand in his mouth. "Another agent was killed. I took a slug but survived."

"I see."

He thought she really might have seen how a state of mind like that had landed him in her kitchen.

"Well, I wanted to tell you how much we all have enjoyed your cooking," she said and reached for her cane as she pushed back her chair to stand.

He rose as well, seeing that he was being dismissed. "Thank you."

"What did she want?" Enid demanded the moment he stepped into the kitchen.

He suspected she'd had her ear to the door and had heard most if not all of what had been said. "She wanted to know what I was doing here." He shrugged.

"And what did you tell her?"

He repeated what he'd told Pepper and Enid grunted, clearly unimpressed that he was a government agent, preferring to believe this was about his pregnant girlfriend.

"Like it is any of her business," the cook said, making him want to laugh. Enid was much nosier than her employer.

LIZZY RODE BACK TO THE McCormick Ranch, wondering if there was a chance

Waters had been telling the truth about why he was in Montana. He'd said it was extortion. Clearly Janie had been blackmailing Worth Winchester.

If the two were connected, then why hadn't Waters admitted it?

He likes playing games, she thought. Did he not realize that he was considered a rogue agent and that his little trip to Montana had put him in danger from his own organization?

She remembered the call she'd gotten from Roger Collins giving her the assignment. He'd been perfectly clear: agent TD Waters was to be considered armed and dangerous. He had left against orders. He was considered a rogue agent and because he was highly classified, extreme measures might be needed.

What had TD Waters done prior to coming to Montana that had led the agency to believe he'd gone rogue? She needed more information and yet she knew it wouldn't be coming from Roger Collins. Her job was to report on Waters's activities and to stand by for further orders.

Lizzy had always done as she was ordered. Because she looked harmless, she'd been an asset to the agency on those jobs that required finesse, her boss had told her.

"They don't see you coming," Collins had once joked. "You're like a stealth bomber."

Had TD Waters seen her coming? There was no doubt that he was suspicious of her. She had to wonder what his idea of "joining forces" entailed. She could only imagine after that kiss.

But if she hoped to get the information her boss wanted, then she had to get closer to Waters—no matter how dangerous he was.

As she topped the hill, the barn and stables below her, Lizzy spotted Janie. She was coming out of one of the outbuildings at the back of the property. Reining in, Lizzy waited until Janie passed through the barn and headed for the house before she rode down to the outbuilding.

As she slid off her horse, she noticed that the door to the outbuilding was padlocked. Her suspicions rose as she tried to look into the dirty windows and saw that they had been covered with cardboard from the inside. What had Janie been doing in there?

And what was it she didn't want anyone to see?

The padlock would be fairly easy to pick with the right tools. Lizzy looked over her shoulder and realized she could see the second floor of the main house past the barn—and therefore could be seen, as well. Anne or Janie could be watching her right now. She'd have to come back tonight after everyone was asleep.

Stepping away from the outbuilding, she swung back up onto her horse. As she rode toward the stable, she couldn't shake the feeling that she was being watched.

Chapter Eight

As TD helped make more pies for dinner, he was anxious to track down the Whitehorse Sewing Circle. He could only assume the reason he'd been given that second clue was because he'd been one of the babies the circle had adopted out.

So why hadn't he received a quilt if every baby got one, he wondered? Or had his "parents" gotten rid of it so they never had to explain where it came from?

He knew he was mulling all this because it beat thinking about his run-in this morning with Lizzy Calder—and that kiss. How had he expected her to react?

Maybe a little more friendly.

Come on, Waters, she isn't like the other women you've run across.

No, she wasn't, was she? That's what made her so interesting, and probably why he was going through hell trying to keep her out of his thoughts.

What worried him was the feeling that she knew a lot more about all this than she was letting on. That, coupled with the fact that he was certain she'd recognized him the first time they'd seen each other, had him concerned. Was it just a coincidence that they both ended up here at the same time?

He realized he knew nothing about her. Where was she from? What did she do for a living? Was she from Montana?

After he got the pies in the oven, he wandered down past the living room. He'd seen a computer in a small room near the parlor. The house was deathly silent. He noticed that one of the ranch pickups was gone and wondered who'd left.

Seeing no one around, he slipped into the small room and closed the door quietly behind him. It didn't take long to call up a private information site that required him to use his password. He knew it would alert Roger Collins, but he had no doubt that Collins already knew where he was—that Collins knew a whole lot more than he did.

TD typed in the name Lizzy Calder. Nothing.

He realized his mistake and typed in Elizabeth Calder. Again nothing.

That couldn't be right. He went to a general site and typed in the name. A dozen Elizabeth Calders came up. He began clicking on each. Most were the wrong age. Only one fit. He found a high-school photo. Bingo.

She'd gone to a fancy boarding school. That surprised him.

College, another expensive and prestigious school. She'd earned her degree in business management. Seriously? And now she worked as a consultant?

So why was he having such a hard time believing that? Maybe because his own background read something as bogus along the same lines? Or because it didn't quite fit the woman he'd first seen riding that chestnut mare as if the devil himself were chasing her?

PEPPER HAD ALWAYS BEEN good at sizing people up. She'd had a lot of experience as a young girl working with her father as they traveled with the carnival. In fact, she'd been so good, her father had sent her out in the crowd from the time she was little to bring back the suckers to his carny booth.

She had sized up TD Waters from the first

time she'd seen him and was glad that she hadn't been wrong about him. It worried her a little that he was a government agent, especially with Worth staying here.

Her son Worth had sworn the trouble he was in had nothing to do with drugs. But that didn't mean he hadn't lied. He'd also sworn he wasn't in trouble and any fool could see that he was.

As if she had conjured him up from her thoughts, Worth suddenly appeared in the hallway ahead of Pepper.

"I was just looking for you," Pepper said, taking him by surprise because clearly it had been the other way around. "Why don't we step into the parlor?"

He moved aside to let her lead the way. She could almost feel his relief. He'd been about to confront her. She'd seen his expression and she'd known it would have gotten ugly.

"I have been thinking about your request," she said the moment he'd closed the door. She hadn't bothered to sit down because she knew this wasn't going to take long.

"I called for an appraisal on the ranch but I can't get one until after the holidays," she said.

"I need—"

"Money before that." She nodded and reached into her pocket and pulled out her checkbook.

He sighed and slumped into a chair. She thought for a moment he might cry, his relief was so evident.

Pepper moved to the small desk in the corner and took out a pen. She took her time writing the check. Out of the corner of her eye she saw that her son had his head in his hands. She thought for a moment that he was weeping.

She knew she should pity him but all she felt was disgust. He was weak and she couldn't abide weakness. Even as a young girl, she'd learned that she had to be tough, she couldn't give in to weakness. Her life traveling the country with her father hadn't been easy, far from it. She'd been made to do things she abhorred, pulling in naive young men by using her looks so her father could fleece them at his carnival booth. She had watched them lose their hard-earned money and felt sick to her stomach that she'd had a hand in it.

"It's their choice," her father used to say when she'd argue that she didn't want to do it anymore. "You didn't hold a gun on them. They might as well learn early on that letting a pretty girl turn their heads is going to cost them. This is how we put food on our table.

You don't like it, when you're old enough, you can leave. Until then, get back to work."

As Pepper finished writing out the check, she closed her checkbook, put it back in her pocket and replaced the pen before she got to her feet.

"Mother, I..." He couldn't seem to find the words.

She held out the check.

He took it, looked at the amount, his gaze darting back up to hers. "It's only for ten thousand," he said, sounding both shocked and angry.

"I'm sure that will hold you over until the appraisal comes in," she said even though she'd anticipated just the opposite.

"I told you that I needed fifty thousand," he said, visibly shaking.

She simply looked at him for a moment, wondering if she was to blame for all of his shortcomings. But she couldn't imagine that she'd had that much of an influence on any of her children. She'd always thought of them as being Call's. Except for Trace. He had been hers.

She held her hand out for the check. "If you don't want it..."

He quickly folded the check and put it in his shirt pocket but the look he gave her was like a poisonous dart. Good thing she was immune to her children's hatred or it would have killed her by now.

As he turned to storm out, she thought about warning him that there was a government agent in their midst, but she held her tongue.

She was disgusted with herself for giving him even ten thousand dollars. But she had to make sure that he did nothing to ruin McCall's wedding. If he thought she was calling an appraiser, then he wouldn't want to blow his chance to get what he considered his fair share of the ranch.

If the trouble he was in could just hold off until after the wedding.

"What did he want?" Virginia asked, coming into the room Worth had just deserted.

Pepper gave her an impatient look.

"He wants money, doesn't he?"

"Don't you all?" She regretted the words at her daughter's hurt expression. "I'm sorry."

Virginia looked surprised, then smiled. "I think that is the first time you've said that and really meant it. Did you ever consider that some of us just want your love, your respect?"

"What do you have planned today?" Pepper asked, wanting to change the subject. She'd never understood her daughter. Virginia was too needy, too clingy and always had been. Pepper could blame herself for the way her daughter had turned out, but there was nothing she could do about it now. While they'd grown closer over the past few months, she knew that nothing could fill that gaping hole in Virginia that her daughter had spent years trying to fill through affairs with rich men and alcohol.

"I have to go into town. For my sanity," Virginia said, clearly disappointed in her mother. That, too, was nothing new.

Pepper had never asked what Virginia did in town, whether it was business or frivolity and boredom that took her into Whitehorse so often lately.

She didn't ask now. She'd abandoned her adult children, forcing them to fend for themselves or perish. Her son Angus had perished, killing himself with alcohol. Brand had survived, raising his two sons on the road, but apparently never finding love. Virginia and Worth, well, who knew about their personal lives. They were both mysteries, ones she didn't feel up to solving.

"Enjoy yourself," was all she said as she headed for the kitchen. Right now she was much more curious about what TD Waters was up to.

But when she reached the kitchen, Enid told her that TD had left to run an errand and wouldn't be back until supper.

An errand? "Did he say—"

"Wasn't none of my business," Enid said pointedly. "Ain't none of yours either."

"Aren't you afraid that one day you will push me too far?" Pepper asked.

"Nope. No mystery at all why I'm not. Shouldn't be to you either."

Enid amazed her sometimes. Pepper remembered the first time she'd come to the ranch as a newlywed. She'd inherited Enid and her husband, Alfred Hoagland. Enid had been younger than herself. Alfred older than both of them.

Even back then Enid had been sure of herself. She'd been hired by Call's parents and had acted as if it would take dynamite to get her off Winchester Ranch. You'd have thought she was a Winchester the way she bossed everyone, including Pepper.

Over the years, Enid had become as much a fixture as the log lodge itself. She'd always been there, always listening, always butting her nose into everyone's business.

Pepper regretted that she'd let Call talk her

into letting Enid stay. And after Call disappeared, it had been too late. Enid knew too much about the family, too much about Pepper herself. Enid wasn't going anywhere.

She thought now about the days after she'd lost Trace, twenty-seven years ago. At one point, Enid had drugged her, keeping her in a foggy state that she hadn't minded—in fact, she had welcomed the oblivion.

That was until her only granddaughter, McCall, had come into her life and she'd found out that Trace hadn't run off as everyone had said—but had been murdered. Suddenly she'd had a purpose for living. She'd stopped drinking the tea Enid brought her. She'd stopped eating any food she hadn't seen prepared. And Enid had gotten the hint.

But Pepper still didn't trust the woman and knew that one day she would have to get rid of Enid.

Enid thought she held all of the cards in this game of life or death. But what if Pepper now knew Enid's secrets and had changed the game?

Pepper smiled at the wiry old woman. "I wonder what I'll do without you, Enid." She left the kitchen, but not before glancing back just once.

Enid had the most priceless look on her

face that Pepper had ever seen. It felt good to give the mean old woman some of her own medicine.

"WHERE HAVE YOU BEEN?"

Janie startled her. Lizzy hadn't seen her as she'd entered the house but now realized that Janie had been lying in wait for her. Heart pounding, Lizzy asked, "I beg your pardon?"

"It was a simple question. Where have you been?"

"I went for a ride."

"You've been doing that a lot since you got here. Where did you ride to?"

"Why do you care?"

A hard gleam came into Janie's eyes. "You followed me."

"Why would I do that?" Lizzy demanded and tried to step past her.

Janie grabbed her arm. "Don't ever follow me again."

Something curled in her stomach like a cold-blooded snake. It would have been so easy to free herself from Janie's biting grip. So easy to resort to her hand-to-hand combat training. So easy to take Janie down and wipe that sneer off her face.

Lizzy bit down on her anger, reminding

herself what was at stake here. "As I said, why would I follow you?"

"Be careful, Lizzy, I think you've forgotten how dangerous it can be on a ranch. Accidents happen all the time. I would hate to see anything happen to you."

She was too stunned to speak at first. "You aren't seriously threatening me, are you?" The words seemed to catch in her throat. This was Janie, Anne's sister, a girl she'd known all her life.

"Threatening you?" Janie asked with a laugh and stepped closer. "If I was threatening you, you would have found a rattler in your bed this morning. Your saddle cinch would have snapped on your ride. Your breakfast would have had just enough poison in it that you would have nearly died."

Lizzy stared at the woman in horror.

Janie laughed again. "So in answer to your question, no, I'm not threatening you, Lizzy. I hope I never have to threaten you." With that she turned and left the room.

TELLING ENID HE NEEDED to run an errand before supper, TD went first to his cabin and showered and shaved, changing into jeans, boots and a Western shirt. He grabbed his Stetson as he headed for the door.

Enid had given him directions to Old Town Whitehorse, where the Whitehorse Sewing Circle had met for years to make quilts for each baby that was born—and run an illegal adoption ring.

"Who should I talk to?" he'd asked Enid.

"Pearl Cavanaugh. She's still the head of it. She's had a stroke and she's old as the hills, but don't let that fool you. She's sharp as a tack and as powerful as any woman in this area, except for Pepper Winchester."

"You sure she'll talk to me?"

Enid had studied him for a moment. "This woman you've knocked up, you love her?"

He realized this was where he had to lie and let her keep believing he'd gotten some poor soul in trouble. "It was one night, I was drunk, she was drunk—"

"I get the picture. Pearl will help you as long as the woman is willing to give up the baby."

"She's already got four kids, all under the age of eight."

Enid gave him a pitying look. "All with different fathers I'd wager. You aren't real bright are you."

He'd shrugged and she had shooed him out of her kitchen, saying he'd best take care of his errand.

Now as he came out of the cabin, he glanced in the direction of the lodge. He hadn't seen Worth Winchester since early this morning when he'd been headed for one of the pickups parked out front. He'd been surprised when his brother Brand had joined him in the truck and the two had driven away.

Virginia Winchester had left earlier to go into town. He wondered where they were all off to—and which one of them was leaving him the clues to his past?

It seemed odd he hadn't been pressured into forking over the fifty grand yet if his extortionist was Worth Winchester. Clearly the man was in a bind with his blackmailer demanding twenty-five thousand from him. Maybe he was wrong and the person who'd gotten him to Montana wasn't Worth.

And maybe this wasn't about the money at all. That thought scared him more than he wanted to admit. An extortionist he understood and could handle. The other…well, that made him wonder what that person really wanted from him if not money. He feared the price might be much higher.

LIZZY FELT A COLD DRAFT of air as she stepped into the room and saw Anne hunched over the desk. She hesitated, considering how much she should tell her.

"Anne? *Anne?*"

Her friend turned, instantly appearing irritated. "Now really isn't a good time, Lizzy. I was just going over the ranch bills."

"I'm sorry to bother you, but I need to talk to you about Janie."

Anne sighed. "I told you that you being here would upset her. This whole thing with Mother..." She sighed. "What did she do?"

"She threatened me."

"Janie threatened you?" Anne sounded disbelieving. Even more than that. She made it sound as if Lizzy had made it up to cause trouble. "I'm sure she wasn't serious." She turned back to what she'd been doing at the desk.

"She was serious. Anne, I'm worried about her." Lizzy knew she had to tell Anne everything and yet hated to admit that she'd followed her sister.

"Janie left the ranch early this morning on horseback. I followed her."

Anne turned around again, her brows shooting upward in both surprise and annoyance. "Why would you do that?"

"She's been acting so...oddly. I was curious where she was going at that time of the morning. We both know she isn't an early riser. She also hasn't shown any interest in riding horses from what you said."

Lizzy could see that Anne resented this. How dare she question Janie's comings and goings?

"She rode over to the Winchester Ranch."

Anne sighed. "You know we've always ridden on their land."

"But this time she met with one of the Winchesters."

Her friend froze. "You have to be mistaken."

Lizzy realized how tired she was getting of Anne no longer trusting that she was telling the truth. "She met Worth Winchester. I'm sorry, but I overheard their conversation—"

"Stop."

"Anne, it sounded as if she was—"

"No, I said stop!" Anne was on her feet. "I said that's enough."

"—blackmailing him."

Anne's face turned to stone. "I think it would be best if you left. I told you this was a bad time for a visit."

Lizzy couldn't believe her ears. "I just told you that I overheard your sister blackmailing Worth Winchester. She was demanding twenty-five thousand dollars. Anne, I got the feeling that he could be dangerous if pushed into a corner and apparently he is having trouble raising the money."

"I don't want to hear any more of this. It's ridiculous. You obviously heard wrong. I'm appalled that you would follow her in the first place and then eavesdrop on her conversation."

"And I'm appalled that you don't believe me."

They stood glaring at each other.

"You came here expecting things to be like they were when we were kids," Anne said. "Well, I'm sorry, Lizzy, but they aren't. I'm asking you to leave."

Realization sent goose-bump ripples across her skin. "You knew she was blackmailing the Winchesters." She thought about what Waters had told her and knew he was right. "This has something to do with what the sheriff was asking you about. Did Janie see who murdered Trace Winchester? Did you both see the Winchester who was involved?"

She took a step toward the woman she'd thought would always be her best friend in the world, no matter what. "Anne, you can't—" A hand clamped down on her shoulder. Fingers bit into her flesh and spun her around.

"We're through asking you nicely," Janie

said. "I've packed your bags. They're waiting for you downstairs."

Lizzy looked to Anne, but she'd already turned her back.

SHERIFF MCCALL WINCHESTER hated investigating her own family, but when she spotted her aunt, Virginia, in one of the ranch trucks headed south, she decided to see what was up.

As far as she knew, Virginia hadn't left the ranch but to go into town since she'd arrived months ago. Now her aunt was headed south and McCall had an eerie feeling she knew where she was going.

Miles south of Whitehorse, Virginia turned down a road all too familiar to McCall. Her heart lodged itself in her throat as she drove on past, then doubled back. Parking off the main road where her patrol car couldn't be seen, she circled around on foot and climbed up the side of the ridge.

The hike up the steep, snowy hillside was a painful reminder of last spring, when she'd climbed up this ridge after a thunderstorm. The storm, known in these parts as a gully washer, had washed some bones down from a shallow grave on the ridge. A local rock collector had found the bones and called it in.

McCall had gotten the call and, after her climb up to the top of the high ridge, had discovered the shallow grave—and a piece of identification of her father's. Ultimately, her investigation had led her to at least one of the people responsible for his murder. The only missing piece was what the killer had told her moments before dying.

Someone in the Winchester family had been involved.

Now as McCall neared the ridgeline, she slowed, hearing another vehicle. A pickup door slammed. As the second vehicle engine died, another door opened and slammed. Then another person got out of the second pickup.

She stayed where she was. Last spring on the day she'd found her father's grave, the wind had howled across this ridge. Today, though, it was still and quiet, so still and quiet she was easily able to recognize the voices of the three people on the ridge. Just as she was able to hear what they had to say.

McCall laid back against the hillside, her heart in her throat, as she heard Virginia and her brothers, Brand and Worth, arguing over which one of them had been in cahoots with their younger brother's killer.

Chapter Nine

As TD left the ranch, hit the county road and headed south, he spotted a car coming down the road toward him. It surprised him to see another vehicle this far from civilization, especially one coming up from the badlands of the Missouri Breaks.

His real surprise came when he recognized the person behind the wheel.

He hit the brakes and rolled down the pickup window as Lizzy pulled alongside. From the expression on her face something had happened and it wasn't good.

"You all right?" he asked as she whirred down her window.

"I tried to talk to Anne about her sister."

"I take it that didn't go well."

She attempted a smile.

"So where are you headed?" he asked, spotting her overnight bag in the back seat.

"I hadn't thought that far ahead."

"Park your car up the road in that spot where the plow turned around and come with me."

"Where are you going?"

"Old Town Whitehorse. I told you I was up here because of an extortionist? If you want to hear the whole story, you'll have to ride along. Don't look so suspicious. I'm just going to Old Town to talk to the Whitehorse Sewing Circle. How scary can that be?"

"The Whitehorse Sewing Circle?"

He made a cross over his heart with his finger. "I don't want to go alone." He saw her weaken. "Park. I'll back up and pick you up."

"Tell me you don't think a bunch of quilters are trying to extort money from you," she said as she climbed into his pickup. "Oh, that's right, it isn't about you, necessarily."

He chuckled. He liked her sense of humor. Hell, he liked her more all the time. And he'd been telling the truth. He hadn't wanted to go to Old Town Whitehorse alone.

Of course, taking her with him to Old Town probably wasn't his best move. As if he'd been thinking rationally since he'd gotten that phone call in the middle of the night. He'd been winging it. Just as he had when he'd invited her to come along with him. He couldn't let her leave, and maybe showing up with her might actually work to his advantage.

Or put her in danger. He let out a silent curse. He'd just have to make sure she stayed safe, wouldn't he? As he glanced over at her, he got the feeling though she might be able to take care of herself just fine.

LIZZY SNAPPED ON HER SEAT BELT. Waters was driving an older model pickup. She was guessing he'd paid cash for it, thinking it would make it harder for the agency to find him. Or at least take them longer to find out what he was driving.

As she glanced over at him, she wondered if he really did not realize that Roger Collins had known where he was heading almost immediately. Or that Roger knew this area? Still, that wouldn't explain how he knew TD Waters was headed here.

"I'll tell you all about the extortion, but first tell me about your run-in with the McCormick sisters. Bad fight?"

"Uh-huh." She hesitated to tell him, but then realized he already knew most of it. "What hurts is that I realized my friend Anne already knew that her younger sister, Janie, was blackmailing Worth Winchester. Or at least suspected. The two of them could even be in on it together."

"So they did see who from the family was involved in Trace Winchester's murder?"

"Apparently it was Worth and they're blackmailing him."

TD didn't say anything for a few minutes as he drove. It was a beautiful winter day in Montana. The massive sky overhead was robin's-egg blue, the sun almost warm coming in the pickup's side window. Only a few puffs of clouds dotted the horizon and the snowy landscape seemed to be covered with diamonds.

"I get the feeling that there is more going on," she said, remembering the locked shed. "Maybe you should warn someone at the Winchester Ranch."

He shot her a surprised look, then shook his head. "I'm just helping cook there."

"I still can't believe you cook."

"Why do you sound so surprised?"

He didn't seem like the type and she said as much.

TD laughed. "And what type do you think I am?"

She knew better than to touch that with a ten-foot pole, as her father used to say. "You're more of a cowboy."

"Like cowboys can't cook?"

"Not the ones I've known."

"Clearly, you have known the wrong cowboys," he joked.

Lizzy was still trying to digest the fact that he apparently had hired on at the Winchester Ranch to help cook. "So you're helping cook, kind of undercover, as you try to find this extortionist?"

He shot her a look, picking up on her sarcasm, and for a moment she thought she'd gone too far. "The truth? I'm trying to find out who I am."

"Couldn't you have just taken a drumming class?" she joked.

"I think I might have been adopted, possibly through an illegal adoption. More than actual extortion, someone is trying to get me to pay for information about my birth."

"I'm sorry." She stared at him, wishing she hadn't made light of it moments ago. "So your parents..."

"Weren't really my parents maybe."

She thought of the framed photograph, the different name on the back. "And you think this Whitehorse Sewing Circle..."

"Is a front for an illegal adoption ring." He nodded at her surprise as he drove down the narrow road deeper into wild country.

Neither of them spoke for a few minutes.

Lizzy was trying to make sense of this. If TD Waters was telling the truth, he was anything but a rogue agent. Why had she been sent after him if all he was doing was trying to find out the truth about his birth?

Because the truth had larger consequences that would somehow affect the agency? Or affect their boss, Roger Collins?

She thought of the photograph, proof that Collins had been in this area. Proof that he'd known her father. Was there some reason he didn't want Waters to find out who his birth parents had been?

"There it is," TD said as he slowed the pickup. "Old Town Whitehorse."

She looked out the windshield at what at first appeared to be a ghost town. She'd heard of Old Town, the first town of Whitehorse. It had been nearer to the Missouri River, but when the railroad came through, the town migrated north, taking the name with it.

The original settlement of Whitehorse was now little more than a handful of ranches and a few of the original remaining town buildings. At one time, there'd apparently been a gas station, but that building was sitting empty, the pumps gone.

There was a community center—every small

community up here had one of those—and a one-room schoolhouse next to it.

Past that, there were a few houses, one large one boarded up, a sign that said Condemned nailed to the door, and another with smoke coming out of the chimney—someone was still living there, apparently.

TD pulled in next to the schoolhouse in front of what a sign proclaimed was the Whitehorse Community Center. There were a half-dozen vehicles parked outside, mostly pickups, all four-wheel drives.

"Do you want me to wait here?" she asked, hoping he would say no.

He did. "If you think I'm entering a building full of women armed with needles alone, you're crazy."

"And here I thought you were so brave and courageous," she said as she smiled over at him.

"Whatever gave you that idea?" he asked, sounding serious. "Women scare the hell out of me. Especially ones like you."

"Yeah, sure," she said and popped open her door, warmed by the look in his dark eyes.

"If things go badly in here, I'll be hiding behind you," he joked as they walked to the door.

McCALL COULDN'T BELIEVE what she was hearing. Her aunt and two uncles had started out fighting and accusing each other of being murderers.

At first McCall had wondered if the three of them hadn't done it together, but she quickly chucked that idea when she realized that the way they got along, they would have sold each other out a long time ago.

"Wait a minute," she heard Brand say. "Let me see if I have this right. You both swear you had nothing to do with Trace's murder."

"That's what I've been telling you all along," Virginia snapped. "And you haven't believed me. I might have said I wish Trace had never been born once in front of Sandy when I was angry but do you really think I would have had a part in killing my own brother?"

"She's right," Worth said. "We might have resented him, but I don't think any of us would stoop to murder. What would have been the point? Trace was married to Ruby, who was expecting his kid. He'd moved off the ranch and, let's face it, he and Mother weren't getting along that great. So what was our motive for getting rid of him? The way it looked to me, he was already gone."

"Worth has a good point," Virginia agreed.

"But Mother is positive that one of us was on that ridge and that there was a witness."

"Janie McCormick says she was that witness," Brand said.

McCall shifted her position, suddenly chilled and aware that her pants were getting soaked from lying against the snowy ground.

She heard a gasp, probably from Virginia, then a silence between the three that spoke volumes.

"Janie has demanded that I pay her twenty-five thousand dollars or she will go to Mother and say she saw me on the ridge that day," Brand said.

"She came to me with the same thing," Virginia cried.

"Me, too," Worth said. "I've been trying to raise the money even though I wasn't on this ridge and had nothing to do with Trace's murder. But let's face it, if Janie told Mother it was me, what are the chances she would believe me?"

Virginia let out a bitter laugh. "I paid the bitch for the very same reason."

"I told her I couldn't raise that kind of money if my life depended on it," Brand said, "but I just found out that she went to my boys and they were ready to pay her—not that they believed I had anything to do with their uncle's murder. Like us, they feared I wouldn't be believed."

"That conniving bitch," Worth said. "Why would she lie?"

"Because she saw a way to make some money," Brand said. "Mother's been asking everyone about who was in the room that day and what they saw. It's not exactly a secret that she has suspected one of us. Janie decided to cash in on it knowing that with our relationships with each other and Mother, we would rather pay than try to defend ourselves."

"But if one of us wasn't involved...why would someone think we were?" Virginia asked.

"Because Trace was killed within sight of the ranch," McCall said as she climbed up over the ridge, startling the three of them. "It comes down to why Sandy Sheridan would lure Trace here to kill him. Clearly she wanted someone at the Winchester Ranch to see it."

AS TD OPENED THE DOOR of the community center for Lizzy, he was glad he'd brought her along. He hadn't let himself think about what he might learn here today. Now, though, he realized he might have been better off not knowing and just leaving this alone.

Maybe that was what Roger Collins had been trying to tell him. Was it possible that was all Roger was trying to do—protect him? And that explained all the secrecy? But if that was true, then he really had to find out the truth because someone on the Winchester Ranch knew who he really was.

He'd been scared plenty of times in his life, but nothing like this as the door opened on a gust of wind. A half-dozen heads turned as he and Lizzy stepped in. The women were all sitting around a quilting frame. They had stopped working, needles suspended in the air, as they looked expectantly at the pair of them.

An elderly woman with a cane rose unsteadily from her chair and motioned for the rest of them to resume sewing. They did, and TD thought of what Enid had said about the leader of the group having almost as much power as Pepper Winchester.

"May I help you?" she asked, her voice sounding odd, and he remembered too what Enid had said about the woman having suffered a stroke. One half of her face sagged a little and affected her speech.

"Are you Pearl Cavanaugh?"

"Why don't we step through here." She motioned to the back of the building and didn't wait for a response.

TD and Lizzy followed her. As they did, TD cast a sideways glance at the quilters. They appeared not to show any interest, but he suspected they would be trying to hear every word that was said.

Pearl Cavanaugh closed the door firmly behind them, then led them through yet another door, closing it, as well.

"Even the walls have ears," she said with a lopsided smile.

"Do you know why I'm here?" TD asked, feeling a little confused.

"Actually, I've been expecting you," the woman said as she motioned for them to have a seat.

Enid had made him swear he wouldn't mention her name, so he doubted she had called Pearl to tell her he was coming. Then who had?

Pearl's gaze went to Lizzy.

"This is a friend of mine, Lizzy Calder."

"Yes," the woman said, nodding in a way that made him think she had been expecting Lizzy, as well.

"There must be some confusion." What he was thinking was that the stroke had taken this woman's mind with it—no matter how sharp Enid said Pearl Cavanaugh used to be.

"You came here to find out if you were one of the children we placed," Pearl said.

TD realized that others must come here for the same reason. "I assume you keep records of the babies you place?"

She gave him that lopsided smile again. "Not in the sense you mean. That would be foolish, given the way we do our adoptions, don't you think?"

"How can you keep track?"

She didn't answer, merely kept smiling.

"Are you telling me you can remember which baby went where?"

Pearl sighed. "The problem isn't remembering. It's forgetting. Nor do I like the responsibility of deciding who to tell and who not to tell when someone like you comes to me."

"Look, I'm not even sure I was one of your babies."

"Oh, you were. Whoever told you about us must have also told you that our mission is to find homes for babies with couples who desperately want a child, and, often because of their circumstances, are unable to go through regular channels. That means we have placed a lot of babies with older couples, couples who don't meet the financial requirements of other agencies."

Like his parents? Or the people he thought had been his parents.

"We try very hard to screen the couples, but every once in a while..." She met his gaze and he saw the bad news coming. "We placed you with a couple who'd been recommended to us, the Clarksons."

He felt his heart stop. Beside him, Lizzy tried hard not to show her surprise, but failed.

TD realized he'd come here expecting this woman to turn him away. To tell him that he'd been given some wrong information.

"How did you—"

"That placement turned out to be a mistake," Pearl said. "Those are the hardest ones to live with."

"The Clarksons were murdered."

She nodded and he felt Lizzy's gaze shift to him. He didn't dare look at her for fear he would see pity in her eyes. He couldn't bear that right now and realized he shouldn't have brought her along. He'd just been so sure this was a wild-goose chase.

"Do you know why?" he asked.

Pearl shook her head. "Don't you? Aren't you now involved in the same line of work?"

So he was right. They'd been with the agency and it had gotten them murdered. That explained how Roger Collins had come into his life.

"This person who recommended the Clarksons," TD asked, "was it Roger Collins?"

Pearl's expression confirmed his suspicions even though she said, "We're not allowed to give out that information."

"But you do know who my birth parents are and you are going to tell me," he said, his throat dry as cotton.

Pearl Cavanaugh pulled back in surprise. "Don't you already know?"

"If I knew, then why would I come to you?" he asked, then apologized for his brusqueness.

"It is understandable. You're upset. Am I to understand that you didn't know until now that you were adopted?"

He nodded.

Pearl seemed more than a little surprised. "I'm sorry. I just assumed when I heard you were back and staying at Winchester Ranch that your mother had told you everything."

He felt a chill even in the hot, small cramped room. "My mother?"

"You really didn't know that you're a Winchester?"

He stared at the woman, switching back to his original assumption that the stroke had fried her brain. Getting to his feet, he said, "This was a mistake. Obviously your memory isn't as good as you thought."

Pearl merely smiled, though it seemed sad. "I wish I could tell you who your birth parents are. All I know is that you were born on the Winchester Ranch and one look at you confirms what I suspected when I first saw you as a baby. You're a Winchester. Normally we require that the name of the mother and father of each baby be given to us, but you were a special case."

"How was that?" he asked, telling himself the woman was nuts but he would play along since he'd come this far.

"The person who brought you to us was known to us and swore the mother wanted to give you up because of a hardship."

"And this woman who brought me to you?" he asked, fear making his throat tight.

"Her name is Etta Mae. She's Enid Hoagland's sister. She's a midwife."

LIZZY COULD FEEL TD'S SHOCK and disbelief. But the woman was right; he looked enough like the Winchesters to be one.

As they left, Lizzy could tell that TD was upset. She realized he'd come here thinking Pearl Cavanaugh would tell him something different. Something much different.

"There's someplace I need to go," he said as he slid behind the wheel of the pickup. "Do you mind a little side trip?"

She shook her head as she buckled up. He didn't say anything as he started the engine and pulled away. For a brief moment, she saw a face framed in the dusty front window of the community center. Then Pearl Cavanaugh was gone and they were driving south again, deeper into the badlands.

What surprised her was that he seemed to know where he was going.

She tried to piece together what she'd heard in the small room at the back of the community center. TD was a Winchester? Or at least had been born on the ranch? Clearly, he hadn't know that.

So who was his mother?

Lizzy was still shocked to hear that his adoptive parents had been murdered. He'd apparently known that, though. Murdered, Pearl had said, because they were in the same business as TD? So Pearl knew that he worked for the agency.

And why had she acted as if she'd been expecting Lizzy, as well? She knew news traveled like the wind across the prairie in these small towns. Still, it bothered her, given that both she and Waters had a tie to this area—and to Roger Collins.

She glanced over at him, wanting to reach out to him. His head must be spinning the same way hers was. He'd apparently not even known he was adopted. He said he'd come to Montana because someone had been trying to extort money from him for information about his past. Someone at the Winchester Ranch?

He slowed and she looked up as he turned down a road that was little more than a rough trail—it cut through rolling, snow-covered prairie studded with sagebrush.

As he turned down the path, she saw something lying in the snow just off the road. An old mailbox. The lettering had faded until she could barely make out the name. *Clarkson.* She felt a chill and hugged herself as she looked ahead, half-afraid of what might be waiting for them at the end of the road.

The pickup lurched over the bumps and dips in the road until they came over a rise and she saw what was left of a house. A lone chimney stood against the skyline, blackened as if the house had burned down.

Lizzy shot TD a look. Is that how the Clarksons had been murdered? Where had TD been at the time? And where had he gone after that?

He stopped the pickup, cut the engine and climbed out. Lizzy didn't move. She sat in the pickup, watching him return to what she knew had once been his home. The home where the people he'd believed to be his parents had been killed. She couldn't imagine what might be going through his mind.

All she could think about was the photograph TD had brought with him of the boy and his dog. She realized that this was where the picture had been taken.

A COLD WIND STUNG HIS FACE as TD walked along the edge of the old foundation. Clouds began to crowd the horizon, as dark as his mood. A part of him registered what was happening. The temperature was dropping. A storm was coming in.

If they didn't get back soon, they could get caught in it. In this part of the country, at this time of year, they could get stranded in a blizzard.

But while the storm clouds crowded the horizon, his story here filled his thoughts, forcing out any concern over a snowstorm. He found himself reliving the past, picturing the house as it had been before that day it was devoured in flames.

He'd hoped coming here would help him make sense of everything. They'd been in the same business he was in, Pearl Cavanaugh had said. Roger Collins would have known that. So why had Collins tried to keep him from learning about his past? What could there be in it that his boss didn't want him to find out?

He stood in the cold December wind, watching a storm roll across the wild prairie toward him, and realized that whatever answers there were, they weren't here on this sad plot of land.

The answers, if Pearl Cavanaugh was to be believed, were back at Winchester Ranch—or with the one person this always came back to: Agent Director Roger Collins.

He figured he had a better chance at getting at the truth at the ranch.

Lizzy was waiting for him in the pickup. He climbed in and sat for a moment before he reached for the ignition. Her hand covered his, stopping him.

"Do you want to talk about it?" she asked.

"I wouldn't know where to begin. Until a couple of days ago I believed that the Clarksons were my parents. They were older, true, they didn't look much like me and they weren't great parents. It's funny, looking back I realize I didn't know them very well."

"How old were you when they died?"

"Eight. I grew up here," he said nodding toward what was left of the house. "I used to spend hours down in the Missouri Breaks, just me and my dog." He glanced toward the south and the broken land that eroded into more rugged badlands as it fell to the river bottom.

He looked over at her. "I don't know what to make of any of this. I'm not sure I believe..." He cut himself off with a laugh. "You think it's true?"

"That you're a Winchester?" she asked, studying his face. She smiled. "You could definitely pass for one."

"I feel like someone is jerking me around. How could Pearl not know who gave birth to me that night?"

"My guess is that they don't ask a lot of

questions, as long as they believe the person who brought you to them," Lizzy said.

"Yeah," he said, thinking of the Winchesters' devoted housekeeper and cook, Enid. How convenient that her sister was a midwife.

Chapter Ten

Enid held the phone, her hand shaking so hard she could hardly keep it against her ear. She couldn't believe this was happening. It wasn't possible.

Pearl Cavanaugh's angry voice came through the line, clear as a bell. "You sent that boy here."

"I don't know what you're talking about." She was trying to understand why Pearl was so angry. The Whitehorse Sewing Circle was always interested in unwanted babies that needed a good home. Those old crones thought it was their "calling" and there were always plenty of couples who desperately wanted a baby. The only thing Enid couldn't understand is why the old crones didn't charge. They could have made a fortune over the years.

"You foolish old woman," Pearl snapped. "He didn't even know he was a Winchester."

That caught Enid's attention. "*What?*"

"He came here thinking he was the son of the Clarksons. I just assumed he knew the truth. Why else would he be staying at Winchester Ranch?"

Enid stood still as a statue except for her heart threatening to beat its way out of her chest as she realized what Pearl was talking about.

"TD Waters?"

"You should know better than anyone who he is. It was your sister who brought him to me that night."

She was a stupid old fool. Of course she'd noticed how much TD resembled the Winchesters. But not every dark-haired, dark-eyed, good-looking man was a Winchester. No, just this one, she thought as she suddenly had to sit down.

TD Waters had seemed too good to be true. She thought back to that day when he'd showed up at the ranch. He'd said there'd been a mistake.

"I would imagine he's on his way back there," Pearl was saying. "I suggest you tell him the truth or I will. Maybe you'd better prepare his mother." She slammed down the phone.

Enid winced and, still trembling, hung up.

She tried to calm down but couldn't. Pearl was right. TD would be back soon. She had to move fast.

She reached for the phone book. It only took a few minutes to find out that the person the employment agency in town had sent out had never made it. No surprise either to learn that the agency had never heard of TD Waters.

Enid hung up, her thoughts at war. What was she going to do? Get rid of TD Waters before anyone else found out. Short of killing him, she wasn't sure how to do that. Firing him now so close to the wedding would make Pepper suspicious, even if Enid could get him to leave without ruining everything. Maybe she could make a deal with him.

How had he found out? He must have known something to show up here. He'd played along because he'd been looking for answers the whole time. What had she told him? Too much. He'd tricked her. She'd thought he'd knocked up some woman. He'd played her for a fool. Not that she wasn't a fool.

And now Pearl had let the cat out of the bag, so to speak. From what Pearl had said, he hadn't known anything before he talked to her. Why else would he ask Enid about the Whitehorse Sewing Circle? He'd come here fishing and had just hooked on to the big one: he was a Winchester.

What would he do now? She hated to think.

One clear thought worked its way to the surface. Someone had talked.

Enid thought back to the night the baby had been born here at the ranch. She'd called her sister, Etta Mae, and begged for her help, since Enid knew nothing about delivering a baby. A mistake, she saw now. No one else knew what had happened to the baby after it was born. No one but her sister.

Why would her sister have told anyone? Enid had sworn her sister to secrecy with the threat of death. The answer made Enid groan. Money. She recalled the last time Etta Mae had called. They'd argued about money. She'd known Etta Mae was thinking of selling the information to the highest bidder she could find and selling out her sister at the same time.

Enid tried not to panic. But she couldn't get that last conversation with her sister out of her mind. She must have already sold the information before she called!

"Haven't you got your money from that old sow yet?" Etta Mae had demanded when she'd called. To look at Etta May you'd think that petite, cute, sweet-looking woman was an angel—not the devil herself.

"What's it to you?" Enid had snapped.

"Things haven't been going so good for me. I was thinking you might want to help me out."

"Like things have been going that great for me?"

"Why don't you get some money from your boss? She owes you for all those years you've put in there and all the secrets you've kept for her. Hell, she owes me, now that I think about it. I've kept the Winchesters' secrets all these years. I'd think she would appreciate that."

"As if that thought just came to you," Enid had said with disgust. "If that's the only reason you called me, I've got to get back to work. I suggest you do the same thing. Do I have to warn you what will happen if you open your big mouth? And don't call me for money again."

Enid had hung up, furious with Etta Mae. She'd realized then that her sister wouldn't keep her mouth shut. That meant someone had to keep it shut for her.

But she hadn't acted quickly enough. Etta Mae had talked to someone. Someone here at the ranch?

Enid picked up the phone again and dialed her sister's number. She had to cover her tracks.

"ALL I KNOW ABOUT MYSELF is what I've been told, and I can't even be sure that is true," TD said as he drove away.

Lizzy knew that feeling. She couldn't help thinking of the photograph of her father and Roger Collins at the McCormick Ranch. "You have no idea why the Clarksons were killed?"

"None, except that when I was taken away from here, I was told that I was also in danger."

She looked over at him in alarm. "And you still came back here?"

"Had to know the truth," he said with a chuckle. "It's my fatal flaw."

Lizzy doubted TD Waters had any flaws. Her heart went out to him as she saw him glance in the rearview mirror, still looking for answers. He'd been lied to, that much was certain. And now she was lying to him, as well.

She thought about her own childhood. Had she been lied to also?

"What will you do now?" she asked as they drove east, past Old Town Whitehorse and into open country again.

"Go back to the ranch and try to get some answers." He glanced over at her. "What about you?"

She shook her head. What was she going to do? She needed to use her satellite phone and call her boss. She'd put off talking to Roger Collins after finding the photograph. Unfortunately, time hadn't changed the uneasy feeling that had settled in her the moment she'd seen Collins on the horse next to her father.

Lizzy felt TD's intense gaze on her. "What?"

"I was just thinking about the first time I saw you. I would have sworn you recognized me even in that split-second when our eyes met." He frowned. "Did you think I was one of the Winchesters?"

She had trouble lying to him. "It was such a close call and happened so fast...but maybe that's why you thought I recognized you." She reminded herself that lying came with the job and this was an assignment. But she was having a hard time seeing him as a rogue agent.

Just the thought that she could be ordered to take TD in at any time felt like a noose around her neck that drew tighter the more she learned about him. She'd seen how vulnerable he'd been back there and had been forced to fight the urge to reach out to him—and confide her own fear about their boss.

"I suppose that was it," he said, not sounding

convinced. "I was just hoping since you spent time around here in the summers that you might know something about me."

"I'm sorry." And she was. She could see how hard this was on him. They had a few too many things in common: a connection to Montana, a connection to this area in particular and the big one, a connection to Roger Collins. That worried her. All the old questions about why she'd been sent here and why Collins considered Waters a rogue agent nagged at her again.

They reached the spot where she'd left her car and TD pulled over. "Earlier, you said I should warn the Winchesters. What is it you think the McCormicks might do?"

She struggled with her loyalty to Anne even in spite of her friend's betrayal. But after what had happened earlier with Anne and Janie….

"That's just it. I don't know. What I do know is that they're angry at the Winchesters and blame them for what happened to their mother. We know Janie is blackmailing Worth Winchester…" It wasn't just that, she realized. "I also saw Janie coming out of an old shed on the ranch. When I went to check it out, I saw that she'd padlocked the door and covered the windows."

"I don't like the sound of that," he said. "Some of these old sheds have explosives in them. Ranches have always used dynamite and blasting caps to take out stumps."

She nodded, not surprised he was voicing her very concerns.

"Being a blackmailer is one thing, but is there a chance Janie might be violent?" he asked.

Lizzy looked away for a moment. "I once saw her beat a horse that had thrown her. If her stepfather hadn't pulled her off that horse…" She shuddered and told him how Janie had threatened her. "I can't go back there, but I can't leave. I'm afraid Anne's in trouble."

"I need to see what's in that shed," TD said.

"It's too visible from the house during the daylight."

"Then we'll have to go tonight. I need you to show me where that shed is. You'll have to come stay with me."

She felt her eyes widen in alarm. She shook her head even as her brain was telling her this might work out perfectly. Roger Collins would be delighted she'd gotten this close to his rogue agent. "That wouldn't be a good—"

"There are four bunk beds in that cabin where I'm staying. You can take your choice."

He held up his hands. "You have my word I won't do anything you don't want me to."

That was exactly what she feared. "Bunk beds?"

He grinned. "Four. You take your pick."

How could she say no? Like him, she felt she had to find out what was in that shed. She also still had a job to do—even if it was becoming almost impossible to see TD Waters as one of the bad guys.

"HELLO?"

The voice on the other end of the line was female, but not Etta Mae's.

"Who is this?" Edna demanded even though she knew.

"Charlotte."

Etta Mae's roommate. "Where is my sister?"

"Dead."

"What? She died?"

"Got hit by a car. Actually, a bystander said it was a dark-colored pickup."

"When was this?"

"Four days ago. The police asked about next of kin, but Etta Mae had scratched your name out of her address book. I couldn't even read the phone number she had for you and I couldn't remember your name, and knowing how she felt about you, I knew she wouldn't want me to even tell the police she had a sister."

Enid bit back a nasty retort. "You say she was hit by a dark-colored pickup. Did the witness get a license plate or any other information?"

"Not according to the police. Did break the headlight, though, so they're looking for a dark-colored big pickup with the left headlight broken out—or recently replaced."

"Charlotte, you are just a wealth of information," Enid said sarcastically.

"I should tell you, she didn't leave you anything. Etta Mae left me her apartment and everything in it. She said it would be over her dead body before she'd let you have any of it."

Probably Charlotte had whatever money her sister had gotten for selling the information about the baby born twenty-seven years ago.

Enid hung up and went to the window. So the police knew that her sister had been run down by a dark-colored pickup four days ago. Enid studied the dark-colored ranch pickup parked outside the window, the one she'd borrowed four days ago. It was dirty enough she didn't think anyone would notice that the left headlight had been replaced.

McCall was still shaken by what she'd overheard on the ridge earlier today. She hated that her first thought had been that all three of them had been in on it.

She felt bad about that now, but since the time she was old enough to understand, she'd heard stories about the Winchesters—especially her grandmother, Pepper. And now that she'd met her grandmother, she still thought Pepper pretty much capable of anything, including murder, and as they say, the acorn doesn't fall far from the tree.

She reminded herself that her own genes were those of the Winchesters, not to mention Ruby. Had she not become a sheriff, she hated to think what she might have become, and said as much to her fiancé when he met her for dinner in town.

Luke laughed as he reached across the table to take her hand. "There is no one like you, McCall."

"I'm not sure that's a compliment."

"You know damned well it is." He was smiling at her and she wanted to pinch herself. How had she gotten so lucky? "I can't wait to marry you."

"Well, you don't have to wait long. I wanted to ask you..." He looked uneasy. "Do you want to spend the night before the wedding—"

"*Please.* You aren't going to suggest we spend it apart? Not after being inseparable for months, are you?"

He grinned. "I just thought maybe you—"

"Wanted to become conventional just because I was getting married?" She laughed and reached over to cup his strong jaw with her free hand. "I'm not going to change on you, Luke, just because we're getting married. I want to wake up every morning lying next to you."

He rose to come around to her chair. He pulled her up into his arms and kissed her in the packed restaurant. She melted into his arms and his kiss to the sound of applause.

"We're getting married!" he announced as if everyone in three counties hadn't heard.

McCall couldn't take her eyes off him as he returned to his seat. She'd thought about telling him what she'd overheard today on the ridge, but she didn't want to talk about it or what she'd realized. It was too painful. She told herself it could wait until after her wedding, but she wasn't even sure that was true.

"To us!" Luke said raising his glass of beer. "I know it should be champagne but—"

"We don't like champagne. We like beer," McCall said, raising her own glass. They touched glasses with a soft clink, smiling at each other across the table, and she promised herself that she wasn't going to let anything spoil this night with Luke.

"It's going to be a wedding we'll never forget," he said.

Her fear exactly.

AS TD DROVE INTO THE Winchester Ranch, the thought hit him like a brick. He'd been born here. He was a Winchester. Was it true? Of course he'd noticed the resemblance, but it had never crossed his mind…

At the top of the hill, he looked down on the ranch dwellings and felt a start. The yard was full of vans and trucks and people. He slowed, wondering for a moment what was going on.

Caterers and florists and party rental crews were unloading box after box as he drove on past and parked down by his cabin. Lizzy pulled in beside him. As they both got out, they looked back at where all the activity was going on.

He spotted Enid standing outside overseeing the unloading. She saw him and pretended to be busy. "Make yourself at home in the cabin," TD said to Lizzy. "I'll be back in a minute."

As he approached the elderly cook, he saw

her tense. "We need to talk." He drew her over to the side of the lodge away from prying eyes, then checked to make sure no one was within hearing distance.

"You told me that you were on this ranch even before Pepper came here as a newlywed, right?" he asked.

Enid nodded. She looked nervous.

"So you're the one person who should know if I was born here."

"What?" It was a halfhearted attempt to seem surprised.

"Are you the one who called me?"

This time her surprise seemed real. "Called you?"

"Asking for fifty thousand dollars to tell me the truth about my birth mother."

Enid groaned. "Fifty thousand?"

Only the amount seemed to shock her.

"Someone called me from here. Any idea who that might have been?"

"From this ranch?"

"You and I spoke that night after I got the call."

Her eyes widened with the memory. She let out a curse, then seemed to catch herself.

"Talk to me. If anyone knows the truth, I'm guessing it's you."

She looked around as if searching for a way to escape.

"Am I a Winchester?"

He saw the answer in her face. "Fine, if you don't want to tell me, then I'll ask Pepper." He started to step away but she grabbed his arm with her bony fingers.

"I'll tell you. She doesn't know."

"Doesn't know what? Who gave birth to me? Or that I'm a Winchester?"

Enid leaned back against the outer wall of the lodge as if needing support. "She doesn't know you're alive. She thinks you died the night you were born. She thinks you're buried in the family cemetery up on the hill." She motioned to a hill beyond the barn.

His heart felt lodged in his throat. "Who was my mother?"

Chapter Eleven

TD stared at the elderly cook, trying to decide if she was serious.

"It's true," Enid cried. "Pepper Winchester is your mother. She was forty-five when you were born. Rather a surprise to us all. That's the real reason she became a recluse twenty-seven years ago. She was pregnant with you. That's why she sent all her grown children away so that they wouldn't find out."

He shoved back his Stetson and rubbed his forehead. "Pepper? But I thought you told me her husband Call had been dead for forty years or so?"

"Call wasn't your father. He was already dead and buried, so to speak."

"Then who was my father?"

Enid seemed to hesitate. He took a step toward her. She held him off with a look that said she'd been threatened by the best and to not even bother. "Hunt McCormick."

He stared at her aghast. "I was the product of this tragic affair that caused the bad blood between the families?"

"What can I say?"

"How about the truth?"

"I'm telling you the truth," Enid snapped. "But you can't go to Pepper with this."

"Can't I?"

She grabbed his arm again. "I told you. She doesn't know you're alive. She isn't going to believe you."

"I think you'll be surprised." He'd seen the way Pepper had been watching him. Had she seen something in him that reminded her of her other offspring?

"I'm begging you," Enid said, a note of panic in her voice. "Don't do this now. The wedding is tomorrow. Pepper has waited for this day for months. Let her get her granddaughter married, then… You've waited this long. What is another day?"

He looked at the old woman. He knew she was trying to save her own neck. She'd lied about the baby dying and sent her sister to the Whitehorse Sewing Circle to get rid of the infant.

"Why did you let her believe the baby died?" he asked, then realized he already knew the answer. "Money. One more Winchester after the ranch."

"And the fortune that goes with it," she snapped. "But that wasn't the only reason. Look at the bang-up job Pepper did with her other children. She didn't need another one to raise. Not that she was interested in the first place. She didn't even look at the baby, made us take it away."

Because she thought the baby had died.

"What about my father? Was he told I died, as well?"

Enid looked away.

"He never knew I existed?"

"Keep your voice down," she warned. "It's a long story, one I'm sure Pepper will tell you when the time comes."

"I'm sure she'll be real forthcoming about her and her married lover."

"Don't be so judgmental. Things aren't always what they seem," Enid said.

"You can say that again," he muttered. "You aren't planning to hightail it out of here, are you?" he asked her.

"Where would I go?" She sounded defeated, but he wasn't sure he believed it.

"Just in case you were wondering, a friend of mine is staying with me," he told her.

"I saw. I thought I told you to stay away from the McCormicks?"

"She's just a friend of the McCormick family."

Her lips pursed in disapproval. "I won't say anything if you don't."

"I'll wait until after the wedding, but then all bets are off."

ROGER COLLINS PACED IN front of the glass wall that looked out on the city below him. Elizabeth Calder hadn't called in since her first report that Waters was at the Winchester Ranch. Maybe he should have sent someone else, he thought angrily.

No, Elizabeth had never let him down. She wouldn't this time. She would come through for him. She was perfect for this assignment. He had to trust that she could handle TD Waters.

Stepping over to his desk, he sat down. He hesitated a moment before he unlocked the bottom drawer and took out the photograph. Elizabeth had been such a beautiful baby. The Calders had done a wonderful job of raising her.

He noticed how young he'd been in the photo of him holding Elizabeth after she was born—just before he'd handed the baby over to Will and his wife to raise. He frowned, remembering how Will had let him down.

"I don't want my daughter going into your damned secret agency," Will had argued years later. They'd ridden away from the McCormick Ranch so they wouldn't be overheard.

"*Your* daughter?" Collins had snapped. "Have you forgotten whose blood courses through that girl's veins? Or the deal you made for her?"

"She's wrong for your organization. Please, I'm begging you—"

"Don't bother. Nothing you can say will change my mind."

"I can't let you have her. I'm going to tell Lizzy the truth. I'm going to tell everyone."

Collins swore now as he quickly put the photograph back into the drawer and locked it. Will Calder had actually thought he could go back on their arrangement.

He didn't like to think what he'd had to do to stop Will. At least with TD Waters he'd picked the right parents first then found them a child. At least he'd thought he'd picked the right parents. Still, TD had made one hell of an agent. Until now.

Collins had never expected more betrayal. Not all his experiments with forming his own force of agents had worked out, he reminded himself. But enough that he could dispose of those who didn't. Still, he hated losing an agent like Waters. Worse would be to lose Elizabeth.

"Any word from Agent Calder?" he barked into the intercom.

"Nothing, sir. Do you want me to try to reach her?"

"No!" he shouted into the intercom and then began to pace again, unable to shake the uneasy feeling he had. Maybe sending Elizabeth to the McCormick Ranch had been a mistake. He thought he'd covered his tracks. But what if he'd overlooked something?

It dawned on him that his two sharpest agents were in Montana together. If they were to put their heads together… He scoffed at the thought. He'd made sure his daughter had heard all about TD Waters's alleged exploits when it came to women. Elizabeth Calder was too smart to let a man like that turn her head.

But Roger Collins hadn't gotten where he was by taking chances, he reminded himself. Maybe it was time to sacrifice Waters. As much as he would hate to lose him, he also couldn't afford a loose cannon.

LIZZY LET HERSELF INTO the bunkhouse and looked around the small cabin. She'd already searched it and doubted there was anything new to learn here.

His two bags were on the top bunk, tucked back from the edge. She took a quick look, not surprised that he'd hidden the weapons he'd brought. Either that or they were in his pickup.

She glanced out the window to make sure he wasn't coming back for anything before she took a look in the other bag. Just clothing, like before.

That's when she realized what else was missing besides the weapons.

The framed photograph.

She found it on a small wooden ledge by the bottom bunk. Picking it up, she sat down on the bed and studied the young boy. She'd been right. The photo had been shot near the house where TD had taken her today.

So it had to have been taken prior to his adoptive parents being killed. For some reason, the thought gave her a chill.

Although he was smiling into the camera, there was something in his eyes that made her sad. She wondered about his childhood, about the man he'd become. Her image of him was so different from the rogue agent that she'd come to Montana to find.

Lizzy was so lost in thought that she didn't hear TD return.

"What are you doing?" His voice was sharp.

She dropped the framed photograph. It hit the floor, the glass shattering. "I'm sorry," Lizzy cried as TD rushed to pick it up. "I was just looking at it."

"No, I'm the one who is sorry," he said, rising with the photograph, the frame broken as well as the glass. "I shouldn't have startled you. It's just that…"

"I had no business touching anything of yours," she said as she watched him dump the broken glass into a wastebasket. "Maybe I shouldn't stay."

"No. This is my fault. This photograph is all I have from the first eight years of my life. It has little sentimental value. I'm not sure why I've hung on to it."

"I noticed it was taken at the old homestead where you took me today," she said.

He looked up at her. "You have a good eye." He was watching her now in a way that made her realize she'd messed up worse than dropping the framed photograph. Her pulse leaped at her mistake, but she tried to hide it as she turned away to look at the bunks on the opposite wall.

A part of her desperately wanted to tell him the truth about who she was and why she was here. But first she had to talk to Director Collins. She had to be sure.

She could feel the heat of his gaze on her. When she turned toward him again, his dark eyes were guarded. Lizzy mentally kicked herself for making such an amateurish mistake. She'd been too interested in the photograph—and his past—and now TD Waters was acting like an agent again and was suspicious as hell of her.

"Look, I'm sorry, I'm a little jumpy," TD apologized as he studied Lizzy. For a moment there… No, he was still shaken by what Enid had told him. He couldn't trust his feelings, let alone his instincts.

And he realized he had feelings for Lizzy. He didn't just like her, he wanted her. And never more than he did right at this moment. She looked upset, scared almost.

"Hey, it's all right, it's just a picture frame," he said, taking her shoulders in his hands as he smiled into her beautiful face. "It was old and needs to be replaced anyway. I've just never got around to it."

She nodded, and kissing her again seemed like the only thing to do. Her lips trembled under his. He drew her closer, breathing in her sweet scent. He couldn't remember ever wanting a woman as much as he did this one, and yet he held back, kissing her gently, lovingly.

That thought made him draw back. He cared about this woman. The last thing he wanted was to put her in harm's way. And yet he'd stupidly invited her to stay with him. What the hell had he been thinking? Collins would be sending agents after him to bring him in. Or more likely, to make sure he disappeared for good.

But he couldn't send her away. Not yet. He'd have to protect her until he knew for certain what the McCormicks were up to. It would be dark in a few hours. With all the people running around the ranch right now getting ready for the wedding, no way would any agents after him make a move. They would wait until tonight. But tonight, TD would get Lizzy out of here. She would take him to that shed. After that, he'd send her to town and out of harm's way.

"Look, I have to go help in the kitchen, but I'll be back," he said. "You should be fine here until I get back, right?"

She nodded, even smiled. "I'll be fine."

"Good." He wanted to kiss her again but there wasn't time. "Tonight we'll check out that shed. I'm afraid you might be right about the McCormicks being up to something. If they wanted to cause trouble, McCall Winchester's wedding at the ranch with all of the family in attendance would be the perfect place."

"Did you speak to one of the Winchesters?" she asked.

"I decided to wait until after the wedding tomorrow." He laid the photo now in the glassless frame on the top bunk, his gaze lighting on the boy's face. Was that boy the son of Pepper Winchester and Hunt McCormick?

How ironic that the only thing he had from the first eight years of his life was this photo of him holding a rifle. Years later when he'd picked up a rifle again, he'd been surprised at how well he shot.

"It was those years hunting deer in Montana," Roger Collins had said after complimenting him on his excellent target-shooting aptitude.

"How did you know I used to hunt deer?" he had asked.

"I just assumed, growing up in Montana like you did."

Collins had looked uncomfortable. How much had the man known about his past? More than he let on, TD thought now.

Not even Collins knew about the small framed photograph that he'd gotten out of the house before he was whisked away. Some things were best kept secret.

Maybe that's why it had startled him to see her looking at the photograph when he came into the cabin, he thought, studying her. What had it been in her expression that had shaken him so?

If there was one thing he'd learned as an agent, people often surprised you. What surprises did Lizzy Calder have in store for him? he wondered, then swatted away the thought like a pesky fly.

He had let the agency and that life make him cynical and paranoid. Lizzy Calder was just what she seemed.

"I'll get your bags for you," he said. "Top bunk or bottom?"

"Top, I think," she said turning to smile at him.

He smiled back. He liked a woman on top.

ENID WENT BACK TO THE kitchen, her mind awhirl. What was she going to do? She'd put TD Waters off until after the wedding. Maybe she should go to Pepper and confess everything—beat him to the punch, so to speak.

She'd told TD to come over and help her serve dinner tonight. Pepper had insisted on having it catered.

"You and Mr. Waters have been working hard enough," she'd said when she'd come into the kitchen earlier looking for TD. "I'm having dinner catered. Maybe you should think about retiring after the wedding. Or at least taking a long vacation."

"If you're trying to get rid of me—"

"I would use a blunt object," Pepper had said with a small chuckle.

"You wouldn't know what to do without me," Enid had quipped.

Pepper had laughed. "Boy, some days I certainly would like to try."

Enid couldn't help but think about the strange look Pepper had gotten in her dark eyes before she'd left the kitchen. Did she already know about TD?

Normally, Enid would have come up with a plan. Twenty-seven years ago after Pepper had gotten pregnant, it had been Enid who'd kept everyone away so no one knew about her boss's secret. She'd kept all of Pepper's secrets over the years and there'd been many.

It was now time to cash in. Pepper owed her.

Enid fingered the container of pills in her

apron pocket. For years after the baby was born, she'd kept Pepper docile by keeping her drugged. She wondered how many of these pills it would take to put a man like TD Waters down. Too bad he'd brought his girlfriend back with him. It would have been so easy if he'd been alone.

LIZZY WAS GRATEFUL THAT TD had to return to the kitchen to help serve dinner. It gave her a chance to call the agency director.

"I won't be gone long," TD had promised. "As soon as it gets dark enough, we'll check out that shed at the McCormick Ranch."

"Do you think it would be all right if I went for a horseback ride?" she'd asked.

"Promise not to go back over to the McCormicks' without me?"

"Promise."

"Help yourself. I'll make sure none of the Winchesters take you for a McCormick and shoot you."

"I appreciate that, since apparently you are one," she said, glad he saw humor in it. But also aware that when TD found out who she really was, gunplay might be part of it.

She'd saddled one of the horses and ridden to the north, taking the satellite phone with her. On the top of a rise, she'd called Roger Collins.

When he answered, she still wasn't sure what she was going to say.

"Elizabeth." Roger sounded so relieved she felt bad about not calling in sooner. "I was worried about you."

"No need. I just didn't have anything to report before now." She touched her tongue to her lips and could still taste TD. "I need to know why Waters is considered a rogue agent."

Silence. She knew she'd overstepped, but she had to know.

"This is highly unusual, but since I have such admiration for you as an agent, I can tell you this. He has in his possession some classified information that puts the security of our organization and our country at risk."

Classified information?

"I've gone through all of his things and haven't found—"

"This would be a small envelope. I'm sure he has hidden it somewhere. If you find it, do not open it. Do you understand? You would be putting yourself in grave danger if you were to open it."

"Yes, sir, I understand." Until that moment, she hadn't realized that TD Waters had gotten to her. Had she really thought about throwing away her career because the man was one devil of a kisser? Or had it been the vulnerability she'd seen in him as he searched for the truth about his past?

She'd let herself forget something important. He was an agent. A rogue agent.

It didn't matter what TD was doing in Montana. He'd taken off against orders. She had to trust that Roger Collins knew more about what was going on than she did with TD Waters. This is what she'd been trained to do. Follow orders. And that was what she planned to do.

She told Agency Director Collins everything she'd learned. He was so quiet on the other end of the line that for a moment she'd feared they'd been disconnected.

"Sir?"

"I'm here. I'm afraid this attempt to find his past is some kind of smoke screen. Agent Waters knows exactly who he is."

She informed him that she was now staying on the Winchester Ranch with Waters.

"Good," he said, sounding pleased. "You are in the perfect position to find the information before he is able to sell it to the highest bidder. Remember, though, do not open the envelope if you find it. And Elizabeth, be careful. Agent Waters is very dangerous—and very clever. Don't trust him for a moment."

That she knew.

"You've done an excellent job, Agent Calder. I commend you. I'm glad you were able to call back for further orders. Elizabeth, I can give you only twenty-four hours to find this classified material. After that point, I'm afraid, given that Agent Waters has risked a very important government secret by going against orders to return to Montana, I will need you to eliminate that risk."

At first she wasn't sure she'd heard him right. "You don't want me to bring him in?"

"No, it's too dangerous to the security of this country. I need you to make sure Agent Waters is disposed of in such a manner that he never leaves Montana, his whereabouts never disclosed. I can't risk that the information he has in his position will get out.

"Sir—"

"That's a direct order, Agent. If you don't feel you can handle it, I can send someone who can."

"No, that won't be necessary, sir."

"Good. I knew I could count on you."

Chapter Twelve

Lizzy was too shaken to go right back to the bunkhouse. She swung up into the saddle and rode as far north as she could before reaching a stretch of barbed wire. She'd been on other assignments, but none had required her to kill anyone.

Not that she hadn't known the day would come. She'd been trained to shoot and knew she could use a weapon to kill someone if she were required to do so.

But now she had twenty-four hours to find some classified information that Waters might or might not have with him—and then dispose of him.

She had gone back to thinking of him as Agent Waters. It had been a mistake thinking of him as TD. A worse mistake letting him kiss her. But Collins had told her to get close to Waters and she had. Maybe too close.

She could tell that he liked her. More likely

just wanted to get her into bed, since that was his modus operandi with women. For a while, she thought as she rode the horse across the snow-blanketed prairie, she'd believed he felt differently about her than all the other women he'd kissed.

Lizzy cringed at the ridiculous thought. A hawk soared over her head, swooping down into a deep ravine, and she realized it was getting late. She had to get back. Waters would be worried—and suspicious. Also she needed to look for the classified information.

As she neared the ranch, she spotted him standing inside a wrought-iron fence on top of a small hill that looked out over the ranch lodge. Moving closer, she saw that it was the family cemetery. She swung down from her horse and walked the last few yards.

He didn't seem to hear her approach. His head was down. He stood over a small grave with a tiny wooden cross, no name on it. As she drew closer, though, Lizzy saw that someone had draped a chain with a heart-shaped locket over the cross. The cheap locket was now tarnished from years in the weather.

She stared at Waters's strong, broad back and thought of the orders the agency director had given her.

"She thinks I'm dead," TD said without turning around.

Lizzy felt a jolt. She hadn't realized he knew she was there. "Your mother?" she managed to say around the lump in her throat.

"Maybe it would be better if she continued to believe that." He turned to look at her.

She felt a little piece of her heart break off and float around in her chest like a kite cut loose in a strong wind. She didn't know what to say in the face of his obvious torment. Something must have happened while she'd been gone, because he seemed different—morose, sad and almost disappointed.

Lizzy had to fight the urge to reach out to him. How easy it would have been to try to comfort him, to tell him that it would all work out. But she knew the truth was far from that.

He stepped through the gate, closing it carefully behind him. She hadn't moved, could hardly breathe. The weight of what she had to do was like an elephant lying on her chest, and seeing him like this…

"TD." It was the only sound she could get out as his gaze found hers and she looked into his eyes and saw raw need so stark that it triggered a desire inside her that had lain dormant and unknown even to her.

"Lizzy." The sound sent a shudder up her spine.

She raised a hand to ward him off, but she wanted this like she had never wanted anything before. She needed him as much as he needed her.

No, don't do this. Lizzy, stop.

But it was too late. He pulled her into his arms. The kiss sealed the deal. She was lost in the warm wanting of his demanding mouth. Lost in the depths of his dark eyes. Lost to his body as he dragged her to him and wrapped strong, unrelenting arms around her and deepened the kiss.

She didn't remember getting to the cabin. Vaguely she heard the door slam and lock, felt his fingers working at the zipper of her coat, the buttons of her shirt and then his mouth was on her breasts, sucking her nipples into hard aching points.

There was the sound of her jeans dropping to the floor, then the feel of his fingers slipping beneath her panties. She arched against him, feeling the cool air caressing her naked back and breasts, and then he swung her up in his arms and was carrying her toward the bottom bunk.

It happened in a passion-filled haze of stroking and kissing, wet mouths and static-charged fingertips, bodies melded together by a common fire of pleasure and pain and ultimately release. It ended in a rush of panting breath, clutching each other as if the ground beneath them might be torn apart at any moment.

Lizzy lay in his arms, still breathing hard, her body slick with perspiration, her heart a hammer pounding out a death knell. *What have you done?*

She dragged herself from the bunk and moved to her own, grabbing the railing of the top bunk for support. She leaned into it, putting her forehead against the edge of the top bunk, fighting tears, waiting for her years of training to kick in.

It had gotten dark out and the temperature had dropped. The floor beneath her bare feet felt like an ice block and the air in the room sent goose bumps exploding over her naked body, rippling across her skin and making her shiver.

Her arms trembled as she slowly slipped her hand into her bag, wrapped her palm around the grip of the pistol…

Behind her, she heard TD get up from the bunk. But he didn't move toward her. She turned around, pointing the weapon at his chest. The tiny red dot of the laser moved restlessly just over his heart.

She steadied it and met his gaze. For one startled moment, she felt her resolve fail her, but when she spoke, her voice sounded stronger to her ears than she felt. "I'm Agent Elizabeth Calder. I'm going to have to take you in."

TD Waters looked down at the laser now settled at heart level, then up at her. His smile was sad, heartbreaking. He knew! He'd known before he made love to her.

"You weren't ordered to take me in," he said slowly. "You were ordered to kill me."

How did he… "Well, I'm taking you in. Whatever you've done—"

"That's just it. You know I haven't done anything except try to learn the truth about who I am." His dark gaze locked with hers. "You're too smart not to wonder why Roger Collins decided that is an act of treason."

"He says you have some classified information in an envelope that you plan to sell to the highest bidder."

TD let out a laugh. "I'm sure you searched my things." His eyes darkened as he must have read the answer on her face. He shook his head. "I never saw you coming. Kudos to

Collins. He definitely picked the right agent to come after me."

"If you just give me the envelope—"

"There is no classified information, Lizzy. Haven't you figured it out yet? I saw you with the photograph of me when I was eight. You're too sharp not to have seen the date and the name on the back of the frame. Who do you think gave me a new name, a new birth certificate, found me foster parents in another state?"

She couldn't speak.

"Roger covered up not only the fact that I was adopted, but why my adoptive parents were murdered, their house burned to the ground. I was too young to understand it all then, but it is clear now. They were agents and he had them killed and me taken away. It is no coincidence that I ended up working for him. You don't still think it was a coincidence that you ended up working for him as well, do you?"

Lizzy thought of the photograph she'd seen of her father and Roger Collins. The laser dot on TD's broad chest began to move as her weapon wavered.

"How long have you known I was an agent?" she asked.

One dark eyebrow quirked. "You aren't the

only agent in this room. I went through your things when I got back from the kitchen. I found the photograph with Will Calder and Roger Collins with their names written on the back. I assume Will was your father?"

That damned photo. She hadn't been able to leave it behind. Just as TD hadn't been able to leave the photograph of him as a boy behind. What had he called it? His fatal flaw. Hers, as well.

She slowly lowered the weapon, glancing down at it as if she suddenly realized if he'd found the photo, he'd also found her gun.

"It's still loaded," TD said, as if reading her mind.

Her gaze flew up to his. He shrugged as if he had his reasons why he hadn't taken out the ammunition.

"How did you know I wouldn't kill you?"

TD let out the breath he'd been holding. "I didn't." His pulse pounded in his ears and he still felt off balance from the lovemaking and believing just moments before that there was more than a good chance he was going to die at the hands of a woman he'd fallen desperately in love with.

"Is that why you made love to me?"

He let out a bark of a laugh as he met her gaze. "I've been wanting to make love with you from the first time I saw you. Once I realized who you were, I knew why you'd been sent here. I didn't want to die before I got the chance to hold you in my arms."

She was still holding the gun, though now it was at her side. Had she expected him to cross the room and try to take it from her?

Instead, he reached for his jeans.

"Roger said if I didn't finish this assignment, he would send someone else," she said behind him.

TD looked over his shoulder at her as he buttoned his jeans. "That means we don't have much time. We need to check that shed you told me about. I'm afraid your friend Janie McCormick is planning something special for the Winchesters," he said as he continued getting dressed.

Lizzy still hadn't moved. He knew from his training how hard it was to go against orders. Like him, she'd been trained not to ask questions. Complete allegiance was demanded and beaten into you.

He suspected that for the two of them it was even harder to disregard a direct order because Roger Collins had had a hand in them coming to the agency. He'd made them both believe he'd done them a huge favor. They were his special agents. They didn't want to let him down.

He turned to look at her as he shrugged into his Western shirt and began to button it. "I know how hard it is to go against orders. Collins handpicked us, made us feel as if we owed him. I know it is almost impossible to let him down."

Lizzy nodded and looked down at the pistol in her hand.

"Collins was right about one thing. There is an envelope he doesn't want getting into the wrong hands," TD said as he finished buttoning his shirt.

Her eyes widened in surprise as she looked at him again.

"After I searched your belongings, I took that old frame off the photograph of me when I was eight." He started to reach behind him but saw her tense. "I was just going to show you what I found. An envelope hidden behind the photo. I had no idea it was there, but it explains a lot. You're welcome to read it."

"You opened it?"

"My parents were agents working with Collins. It was before he became director. It's all in the letter they left me. They must have known once Collins knew they were on to him that he would have them killed. And he did. Collins can't let this letter get into the hands of the proper authorities. He must have suspected they'd left something behind that could incriminate him. That's why he had the house burned down. Fortunately, he never knew about the photo I'd sneaked out of the house. But he must have feared they had left something up there for me. Why else would he be so afraid for me to come here?"

"What are you going to do with the information?"

"Hide it behind the photo again for now until I can get it where it needs to go," he said. "If something happens to me—"

"Don't."

He nodded. "Did I mention who my alleged birth parents are?" He tossed her her clothing.

She caught her jeans in her free hand, her shirt dropping to the floor at her feet, as she looked at him, waiting for the answer.

"Pepper Winchester and Hunt McCormick. Small world, isn't it?"

"Too small when Roger Collins is in it," Lizzy said. He could see that she was reeling from all this.

"You realize there's a target on my back—and now on yours?"

She nodded slowly, then put the weapon

away and he could finally breathe freely again. He watched her pull on her clothing, wanting to stop her and make love to her again. He already knew how dangerous Lizzy Calder could be, he thought, remembering her in his arms. Look how she'd stolen his heart. He couldn't bear to think how this all might end. Right now he just had to check out a shed on the McCormick Ranch, after that…

He pulled on his shoulder holster and grabbed an extra clip for his pistol, then he turned to look across the small cabin at Lizzy.

"Ready?" he asked as he saw her pull on her shoulder holster, grab a couple of extra clips and shrug on her coat.

He smiled to himself. He had to give Roger Collins credit. He'd sent the perfect woman for the job. He'd made only one small mistake: he'd sent a woman with a heart.

Still, if Lizzy hadn't found that photograph of her father and Roger Collins…

Not that he kidded himself that she might not change her mind about the order she'd been given. This wasn't over by a long shot. Lizzy was right. If she didn't follow orders, Collins would send someone who would.

Or maybe that person had already been sent. TD couldn't help thinking about the

McCormicks. After all, Roger Collins had been a visitor on their ranch. What were the chances Lizzy was the only one he'd recruited from there?

LIZZY SAT ON THE PASSENGER seat of the pickup as they drove slowly off the Winchester Ranch. There were no lights on up at the house, no sign of life. The caterer, rental and floral vans and trucks had all left. Stars had broken out all over the huge canopy of sky. Only a sliver of moon graced the horizon. Glancing at her watch, she was surprised at how late it was.

Her skin still felt warm and soft, tingly at even the thought of TD's touch. *You let him get to you.* Is that what happened? Or had common sense kicked in? There'd been red flags. TD and his quest not to destroy the world, but to find out the truth about his past. The photograph of her father and Roger Collins. The feeling she couldn't shake that there was something wrong with this assignment from the moment she learned it meant coming back here.

"Are you all right?" TD asked as he turned down the road toward the McCormick Ranch.

She was still shaken by the letter TD's

father had left with dates and times, enough evidence to put Roger Collins away for life—if he didn't get the death penalty.

"There's a place up here where you can get behind the ranch house," she said, trying not to kick herself mentally for being taken in by Collins.

As TD swung onto the narrow path of a road that followed an old fence line, he turned out the pickup's lights. The starlight shining off the fallen snow made it plenty bright enough to see where they were going.

"Stop up here," she said. "The shed is just on the other side of that draw."

He parked and shut off the motor. They sat in the semidarkness of the pickup cab, the only sound the slow ticking of the engine as it cooled. The night was cold and clear, but when they got out of the truck, Lizzy felt the wind in her face and smelled snow on the December air.

She looked toward the west and saw the bank of clouds huddled on the horizon. A storm had been brewing for some time. With a start, she realized that tomorrow was Christmas Eve. She couldn't help but think about Christmases when she was a girl as she and TD walked through the snow toward the outbuildings in the distance.

She would come back to the McCormick Ranch each Christmas break. Her father and Hunt would decorate the house. Her father used to dress up like Santa Claus and pass out presents to her and Anne and Janie. They all knew who he was, but played along because he seemed to enjoy it so much.

A thought moved through her like the cold December wind. Something Pearl Cavanaugh had said about placing the adoptive children with older couples who couldn't have children of their own. Like her parents.

Where had that thought come from? TD, this assignment, Roger Collins, all of it had her thinking crazy things. *Or was she finally realizing the truth?*

She shook her head, slowing as they reached the back side of the shed. TD had his weapon drawn. She drew hers, as well. Through the cracks in the boards at the back, she could make out a dim light glowing inside the shed.

TD stopped at the back corner of the building, waited for her to take the opposite side, then disappeared out of sight. Lizzy moved as quietly as possible along the dark side of the shed, the whole time listening for any sound inside. As she reached the corner, she hesitated, then took a quick glance. No one in sight in the direction of the house.

She moved to one side of the door. TD did the same. He glanced down at the lock, then at her. Lizzy holstered her weapon and took out her lock picks. TD produced a small flashlight and positioned himself so the light wouldn't be visible up at the house.

It didn't take but a minute once she went to work. The lock fell open. She stepped back, retrieved her weapon and braced herself as TD opened the door.

THE SMELL HIT HIM FIRST. Diesel fuel. Then TD saw the fifty-pound bags of ammonium nitrate fertilizer in the corner. On a makeshift table were blasting caps and a coil of fuse. Under the table was an old wooden box. There were several sticks of dynamite in the box.

He shot a look at Lizzy as he holstered his gun and began to inspect the items on the table.

"She's making a bomb." Lizzy had made the same connections he had. "The Winchester wedding."

"Very good," said a familiar female voice behind them.

TD started to go for his weapon, but stopped

short as he saw that Janie held a gun to Lizzy's head. "Pull that gun and Lizzy dies."

He could only watch as Janie took Lizzy's weapon from her and pocketed it.

"Take his gun," Janie ordered, shoving Lizzy forward.

TD met her gaze, silently warning her not to try anything. One look at Janie's eyes and he'd seen that she was like the bomb she'd been making—a short fuse ready to blow at any moment. He had the feeling she would have loved nothing better than to kill them both right here. Hell, she might have already been ordered to, if he was right about Collins's connection to this place.

So why hadn't she just gone ahead and killed them, he wondered as Lizzy took his weapon and Janie snatched it away, pocketing it, as well.

Because she had something worse planned for them? Or had been given a different order?

"Sit down on the floor," Janie ordered him as she grabbed a roll of duct tape and handed it to Lizzy. "Bind his wrists and ankles. Make it good or I will kill him. Try anything and you can both die here."

Lizzy knelt down in front of TD and he stuck out his wrists, his gaze never leaving hers as he tried to tell her to stay calm and go along for now. Janie was as highly combustible as the ingredients in this shed.

"Bind his hands behind him," Janie ordered and smacked Lizzy hard on the side of the head with the gun barrel.

TD felt anger boil up in him. But if there was one thing he'd learned as an agent, it was not to let emotion make him react in a way that could get not only himself but everyone around him killed.

Lizzy wrapped his wrists and ankles and stood. Janie checked the job she'd done just as Lizzy had expected.

"Janie, what are you doing with all this stuff?"

"Oh, come on, Lizzy. You already guessed it. The Winchester wedding is going to be such a blast." She laughed at her joke.

"These materials are highly combustible and unstable. Anything could set them off at any time and blow up half this ranch."

Janie smiled. "Yes, I suggest you remember that. One misstep from either of you and kaboom."

"You don't want to do this," Lizzy said.

"Do what? You're the ones trespassing on my land. Getting into things that are none of your business."

"Janie, if you go through with this, you are only going to hurt yourself. Look where this kind of hatred and retaliation got your mother."

"Yes, look where it got my mother," Janie said and swung the butt of the pistol.

TD didn't see the blow coming. There was a moment of intense pain, then nothing at all.

LIZZY SCREAMED AND SPUN on Janie, but Janie had anticipated her reaction and back-handed her.

Falling back, Lizzy crashed into the side of the shed and slid to the floor. She saw stars dance before her eyes and for a moment thought she was going to black out. Janie leaned over her and bound her wrists quickly with a piece of tape.

"Try that again and I will blow your boy-friend to kingdom come," Janie warned. "Do you understand me?"

All Lizzy could do was nod. TD had fallen over against the leg of the makeshift table, his eyes closed, a trickle of blood running down the side of his face. She could see the rise and fall of his chest. He was still alive, but for how long? Anything could set off this shed. Maybe that's what Janie had planned.

"Get up," Janie said grabbing her shoulder

and hauling her out through the door. "Make a run for it and I kill you and your boyfriend."

Lizzy heard her padlock TD inside the shed, but there was nothing she could do but bide her time. She could tell Janie wanted her to try something. She wanted to kill them both, but for some reason was holding off.

"We're going to walk up to the house. I sent the hired help home for the holidays, so there is no one here who can save you." She smiled as if way ahead of Lizzy. "You really think Anne would help you even if she could?" She laughed at that. "Let's go."

"Even if she could? Janie, have you done something to Anne?"

In answer, Janie shoved her toward the house. The walk through the cold winter night seemed endless. Lizzy still felt dizzy from the blow to her temple. But it was TD and Anne she was worried about.

Janie didn't bother to turn on the lights as they entered the house. She shoved her toward the open door to the basement. Lizzy almost fell down the dark steps.

"Sorry, wouldn't want you to hurt yourself," Janie said with a chuckle as Lizzy caught herself.

Janie turned on the light to the basement. For a moment Lizzy was blinded as Janie forced her down the stairs. Then she saw Anne sitting in a dark corner of the room. Her wrists and ankles were bound with duct tape. Her eyes were wide with fear.

"Look who's joining us," Janie said to her sister. "And you thought she left."

"Lizzy, I'm so sorry," Anne cried. "I should have listened to you."

"Shut up," Janie ordered. "Or I will put you out of your misery before I'm ready."

"Janie, my God, your own sister?" Lizzy cried.

"My own sister," Janie mimicked. "For a spy I would think you would be smarter than you are. You and I are the true sisters, Lizzy. Don't look so surprised," she said with a laugh. "I've known Roger Collins my whole life. I even knew his mistress, the one he got pregnant with you after having me with my mother."

Lizzy fought to take her next breath. "You're lying."

"Will and your mother were too old to have children. A baby was the only thing missing in their lives," Janie said in a mocking tone. "Remember how your father doted on you, Lizzy? Well, guess what? He made a deal with the devil for your soul. Now what do you think of your perfect father?"

"He wouldn't have done that," she said but there was no force behind it. Hadn't she suspected something the moment she'd seen the photograph of her dad and Roger Collins?

"He made the deal, but he tried to get out of it," Anne said, glaring at her sister. "The day your father died from a fall from his horse, he wasn't alone. I saw Roger ride out after him."

Lizzy felt sick to her stomach. "You're telling me Roger killed my father?"

"You were Roger's daughter and he was determined you would follow in his footsteps."

And she had, just as Roger had planned.

"You weren't Roger's only daughter to go into the spy game. My position is just more special ops," Janie said with a laugh.

Not on the books, Lizzy thought with horror. Roger Collins had set all this in motion years ago. Her, TD, Janie. What had Roger had going in Montana? He was gathering his own select source of children who he would make sure became his private force. Was that another reason TD's adoptive parents had been murdered? They'd discovered what Roger Collins had going on?

"Daddy is so disappointed in you," Janie said to Lizzy, who cringed at the thought that

Roger Collins's blood ran through her veins. "I told him you didn't have what it took to work for the agency. You were too soft, too sentimental, too weak. But he was so sure you would do whatever he ordered you to do."

"Is he ordering you to kill the Winchesters?" Lizzy demanded. "Or is that all your doing? Don't you realize what Roger is doing? He's using you to clean up the mess he's made of things. Just as he tried to use me and TD. But we didn't fall for it."

"How can you speak of our father like that?" Janie demanded.

"My *father* was Will Calder, an honorable man."

Janie glared at her.

"He's going to throw you away, just as he planned to do with TD." But Lizzy could tell that her words were falling on deaf ears.

"It's almost daylight and I have a wedding to attend," Janie said. "It's time to say goodbye." She lifted the gun and pointed it at Lizzy's head. "'Bye, little sis. I'll just tell Daddy that you tried to stop me."

"Janie, please," Anne said. "I'm begging you, don't—"

Before Lizzy could react, Anne threw herself in front of Lizzy. The report of the gun filled the basement like a sonic boom.

"No!" Lizzy screamed as she felt Anne fall back against her and begin to slump to the floor.

Janie was already part of the way up the stairs when she fired two more shots. Lizzy fell beside Anne and lay still. She could feel blood running in her right eye and knew she'd been hit. A few moments later, she smelled the smoke.

Chapter Thirteen

TD woke, head aching, to sunlight streaming through a crack in the side of the shed. He moved and felt the weight of the bomb materials shift above him. He froze.

Careful, he warned himself as he managed to move away from the table. It wouldn't take much to set this whole shed off.

He tried to clear his head. Where was Lizzy? He prayed she was all right and found himself again wondering at the immediate pull he'd felt toward her the first time he'd seen her. At least now he knew that he hadn't been wrong about her recognizing him. But had he known on some level, even then, that it was no coincidence they'd crossed paths?

Last night he'd looked around the shed just moments before Janie had appeared. He remembered seeing some old tools in the far corner. He worked his way over to them and, spotting some rusty wire cutters, turned to grasp them with his hands bound behind him.

Working to get the cutters beneath the tape, he began to saw against the dull blade. He couldn't tell what time it was. Late enough that the sun was up. Everyone might already be at the Winchester Ranch by now. The wedding was to be this afternoon, but the family would be gathering long before that.

The tape finally gave. His hands free, he hurriedly went to work on the duct tape binding his ankles.

That's when he caught the first whiff of smoke. Getting to his feet, he tried the door and heard the clank of the padlock. No surprise; Janie had padlocked it again.

He glanced around quickly. Janie had put cardboard over the windows. Tearing off a piece, he saw that the one window was large enough that he should be able to get through it. Using the wire cutters, he broke out the glass, hurrying now as the smell of smoke grew stronger, reminding him of another house on fire years before. Collins liked to destroy all evidence, he thought as he glanced back at the bomb supplies in the shed, knowing there were more already at the Winchester Ranch. These had been a decoy.

The window opening was small but after

he was able to tear out the sill, he managed to squeeze through and drop to the ground. His head still ached but all he could think about was Lizzy as he ran toward the burning house. The front door was standing open and smoke poured out.

LIZZY WIPED THE BLOOD from her eye and sat up. Janie had set the house on fire. She could hear the flames and smell the smoke. It wouldn't be long before it filled the basement. She touched her temple, felt where the bullet had grazed her and realized how lucky she'd been.

With a cry of both physical and emotional pain, she checked Anne's pulse and found none. Pushing her friend's body off her, she stumbled to her feet, tears blurring her eyes. Her wrists were still bound. She looked around for something to cut off the tape, but seeing nothing, knew she had a more serious problem. Smoke poured from the cracks around the door at the top of the stairs.

She had to get out of this basement—now. She found what had once been an old coal room and found the chute opening. It was now covered with tin. Climbing up on some boxes, she managed to kick a hole in it. She kept kicking, the smoke getting thicker around her as she tried desperately not to think about Anne or worry about TD.

She had to stop Janie from blowing up the Winchester lodge with all of the Winchesters there for the wedding. It was just as TD had feared—Janie planned to take everyone out. Janie was Roger Collins's daughter, and she and Janie were sisters? She felt sick at the thought. Was it true what Anne had said about Roger killing her father?

Anger and pain boiled up inside her. She thought of her boss and the power the man wielded. Too much power and too many people who were at his beck and call.

Finally, the hole was large enough that she could crawl through. She thought again of Anne, dead in the other room, but there was nothing she could do for her.

Lizzy slipped through the hole and dropped into the snow. As she ran around the side of the house she saw flames leaping at the windows—and TD running from the shed. He pulled her to him, holding her so tightly she couldn't breathe.

Then they were racing across the snow to where they'd left TD's pickup. The sun had risen over the Montana prairie, setting the fallen snow ablaze. They saw no sign of Janie as TD drove away. Behind them a huge plume of smoke rose into the perfectly blue sky as the house she'd once thought of as home burned to the ground.

"WHAT ARE YOU doing up here?"

McCall Winchester turned to see her grandmother framed in the doorway of the infamous third-floor room. "I could ask you the same thing."

Pepper stepped in, leaning heavily on her cane. "You should be getting ready for your wedding."

"I wanted to see this room for myself." She raised the small pair of binoculars she'd found tucked into a space below the windowsill. Turning, she put them to her eyes again and looked out the window toward the ridge where her father had been murdered.

"You know who Sandy Sheridan meant when she said someone in the Winchester family was involved in Trace's murder," her grandmother said behind her.

"Yes." McCall didn't turn. She thought for a moment of Sandy, her father's girlfriend whose heart he had broken when he'd taken up with McCall's mother, Ruby—not just taken up with her, but gotten her pregnant with McCall. Sandy had never stopped loving Trace Winchester…or let go of the pain and embarrassment he'd caused her. It had become a love-hate relationship for Sandy.

Probably much like the relationship her father had had with his siblings.

"Which one of my children is it?" Pepper's voice wavered and McCall could hear the fear there.

"It wasn't any of your children."

"But why kill him in sight of the ranch of someone in the family—"

"Sandy Sheridan inferred that someone in the family was involved, but none of them were on the ridge that day," McCall told her, still not looking at her. "They weren't involved, even though you've had them suspicious of each other for months now."

McCall finally turned from the window. "Sandy was referring to you."

Her grandmother frowned and then realization came into her eyes an instant before they flooded with tears. "No!" It came out a cry filled with pain and anguish. "No," she repeated as she slowly slid to the floor.

McCall didn't move to go to her. She had told herself she wasn't going to feel sorry for Pepper. She wasn't going to feel anything, but over the past nine months she'd come to love her grandmother.

She had seen how the past had embittered

her, trapped her in this lodge with no one who cared about her—and one person, at least, who had done her harm.

But neither was she going to try to spare her feelings. "You would have done anything to break up my father's marriage," she said. "I suspect you told Sandy that Trace still loved her, that he was trapped in a loveless marriage, whatever it took to make her think she could get him back if she broke up that marriage. You sent Sandy after my father."

Pepper shook her head, as if denying it would make it all go away. "I didn't know Sandy Sheridan would..." She dropped her face into her hands. Sobs shook her body but no sound came out.

"I couldn't understand why Sandy told my father to meet her on that ridge and killed him there," McCall said, knowing she had to make her grandmother own this. No more hiding in this lodge. No more lying and keeping secrets. It was time for the truth to shine its light not only on her, but also on the rest of the family.

"When he rejected her a second time, she blamed you for putting her through that again," McCall said, remembering the look on Sandy's face just before she died. Now her words made sense. "That's why she killed him on that ridge across from the ranch. Apparently my father had given her the idea because she knew he would be there antelope hunting that day. She was hoping you would see what you had done. She believed that his siblings hated him and wanted him dead as well, but ultimately Sandy was a sick, unhappy individual looking for someone to blame for what she'd done."

Her grandmother raised her head, steel coming back into her spine. Her dark eyes shone from her tears but her voice was strong when she spoke. "I wanted to believe one of my own children capable of murder before I would believe that I had..." She shook her head. "You must hate me."

"No," McCall said as she walked over and sat down next to Pepper. She reached over and took her grandmother's hand. "Have you ever read what is written up here on these walls?"

Her grandmother shook her head. "I couldn't bear it."

"You should read it. I think you'll be surprised and it will help you understand your children better." She rose. "By the way, Janie McCormick has been blackmailing Worth, Brand and Virginia since word got out about your suspicions that one of them was a coconspirator in my father's murder."

"Why would they pay if they didn't have anything to hide?"

"Isn't it obvious? If Janie came to you and said she'd seen one of them on that ridge that day, you would have believed her because you wanted to. Better than the alternative, right?"

Her grandmother had the good grace to lower her head.

"They recently met over on the ridge and realized they'd all been blackmailed and none of them had anything to do with their brother's murder."

"I always said you made a fine sheriff," her grandmother said. "I was right."

McCall took little satisfaction in the fact that she finally knew the whole truth about her father's murder.Sandy Sheridan had loved Trace Winchester—in her own twisted way. True, she probably hadn't needed much encouragement from Pepper to go after him. But when she'd realized she'd been used…

"No more secrets, all right?" McCall said to her grandmother.

"In that case, there is one more thing I should tell you, then." She sighed and leaned her head back to meet her granddaughter's gaze. "Losing your father wasn't the only reason I became a recluse twenty-seven years ago," Pepper said. "I was pregnant."

McCall couldn't hide her surprise.

"I was forty-five. I never dreamed I could still conceive a child. Hunt McCormick was the father."

"What happened to the baby?" McCall asked her grandmother, her heart in her throat.

"Enid and her sister delivered it. I told Enid to get rid of it."

McCall cringed at the thought of what Enid might have done with the baby.

There were tears in her grandmother's eyes again. "Enid told me the baby had died, but I knew better. Her sister left with it. I watched her from the upstairs window. She took the baby to the Whitehorse Sewing Circle."

"How do you know that?"

Pepper merely smiled.

"So I see why you haven't fired Enid. The keeper of your secrets," McCall said.

Her grandmother nodded solemnly.

"Did Hunt know about the baby?" McCall asked, already suspecting the answer.

"No. He had asked me to run away with him." Her old eyes filmed over. "I wanted to, but I was pregnant and I knew Hunt, he'd want us to raise this child. I'd already made such a mess of my other children, I just couldn't."

"You were in love with him," McCall said.

Pepper laughed softly. "He was the love of my life. I met him the first time when I was sixteen. It truly was love at first sight. We would have run away together then, but Hunt was only seventeen and determined to make his fortune. And my father did everything he could to keep us apart. Hunt was headed for the West Coast. But he promised that he would find me and we would be together one day."

"By the time he found you, you were married to Call Winchester."

She nodded. "I had given up that Hunt would ever come for me and by then Joanna McCormick had tricked him into marrying her and refused to give him a divorce. Joanna and I have known each other since we were girls. She was always jealous of me and Hunt and would have done anything to keep us apart. Twenty-seven years ago, I felt it was too late for Hunt and me. The night the baby was conceived was a moment of weakness."

"You know what happened to the baby, don't you," McCall said. "That's why you're telling me this."

"Yes. I found him and got him back to the ranch."

"Are you telling me—"

"TD Waters is my son."

"TAKE THE BACK ROAD, it's faster," Lizzy said as the pickup bounced over a bump.

TD swung down the road, forcing her to hang on. She could feel them racing against time. Any moment the Winchester Ranch lodge might explode in a shower of flames and splinters, killing everyone inside. There'd been enough fertilizer in the shed alone to blow the lodge to smithereens. And apparently Janie had the training, so she knew exactly what she was doing.

Lizzy quickly filled him in on what had happened with Anne and what Janie had told her. He reached over and took her hand for a moment, squeezing it, his look filled with both surprise and compassion when she told him that her father—and Janie's—was Roger Collins.

"Collins started his own little army with young people from Montana," Lizzy said. "I wonder how many more of us there are in the agency?"

"Enough that when there's a problem, a few of us are expendable," TD said as they came over a rise and saw in the distance a McCormick Ranch pickup nearly hidden in a coulee behind a stand of scrub junipers.

TD threw on the brakes and they both jumped out armed and ready.

No sign of Janie. They checked the back of the pickup. They could smell the diesel and the fertilizer and see where she had used a sled to take everything down the hillside behind the lodge.

TD looked over at Lizzy. "You know this place better than I do. The place to put the bomb to do the most damage would be the basement. Is there one?"

Lizzy shook her head. "Just a crawl space."

"That's where she had to put it, then." He didn't have to tell her that the optimal place would be in a corner. In her training, they had piled fertilizer bags in one corner of a basement, piled sandbags around it. When the bomb went off, it had leveled the vacant house they'd used.

She had to assume Janie had gotten the same training.

They dropped off the hillside, coming down behind the lodge. Still no sign of Janie, but Lizzy spotted a plastic sled where it had been discarded behind a bush. As she approached the house, she saw where an air vent had been pulled off along the foundation of the lodge.

TD had seen it, as well. There were tracks in the snow where Janie had squeezed through the small opening under the house. TD moved quickly to it and looked in.

Lizzy knew before he turned to her that there was no way he was going to fit in the crawl space. The lodge had settled over the years. The only reason Janie had been able to was because she was small—like Lizzy.

ALONE IN THE ROOM she'd abhorred for so long, Pepper finally forced herself to read what was written on the wall next to her.

She'd expected the words scratched into the plaster would be cries for help or condemnation of her husband and herself for the lousy parents they had both been.

To her shock, the words were songs or poems. She moved around the room, reading snippets of stories, thoughts, lyrical expressions of children left alone to their own devices.

Had Call ever come up here and read these?

"Mother?"

She turned to find her son Brand standing

in the doorway. "McCall told me to tell you it's time to start getting ready."

For a moment she was confused, so many thoughts and regrets. "Ready?"

"For the wedding? Are you all right?"

McCall was still getting married here at the ranch? She'd thought that her granddaughter would never be able to forgive her. Tears welled in her eyes. She'd thought they would all leave, desert her as she had deserted them.

She smiled up at her son. What a handsome man he was. What a handsome bunch the whole Winchester family was. And they would all be here. Worth, Brand, Virginia, the grandsons and their wives, Cyrus and his lovely Kate, Jack and Josie, Cordell and Raine, Jace and Kayley.

Pepper realized she had to find TD and tell him. He had to be here, as well.

"Yes," she said as she let her son help her up. "The wedding. Don't look so worried. It's going to be wonderful."

WHERE THE HELL WAS TD Waters, Enid wondered as she paced in the kitchen.

She rattled the nearly empty pill bottle in her apron as she paced. She stopped long enough to consider the small carafe of special coffee she'd made him. Maybe she should put in a couple more of the pills. TD was bigger than other men she'd drugged.

"Finally," she said, turning at the sound of the outside kitchen door swinging open. "I was about to..." The rest of whatever she planned to say died on her lips as she stared at the woman standing in the door.

Janie McCormick.

"What are you doing here?" Enid demanded, then felt a chill quake through her as the young woman closed and locked the kitchen door.

"Just tell me where I can find Pepper Winchester, I need to see her."

Enid heard her voice quaver as she asked, "What should I say this is about?"

"Tell her it's about my stepfather."

Enid nodded dumbly. "I'm sure she's getting ready for the wedding."

"Then I suggest you hurry up and find her. I'll be waiting right here," Janie said sitting down and considering the coffee carafe. She grabbed the handle and the cup Enid had put out for TD and was already pouring herself a cup before Enid could stop her.

"Don't drink that—"

Janie gave her a look that said she didn't take orders from Pepper Winchester's maid.

She took a drink, then another, practically gulping it down.

That's when Enid noticed that her clothing looked wet, as if she'd been rolling in the snow. It was also dusty, covered with cobwebs. Where had the woman been?

Janie finished the cup of coffee and started to pour herself another. "Didn't I tell you to get Pepper?" she snapped.

"What's in it for me?" Enid asked, wondering how long it would take for the drugs to take effect.

Janie actually smiled. "So everything I've heard about you is true. I'll give you a hundred bucks to get your boss, how's that?"

"I'll take two hundred."

Janie's smile disappeared in a heartbeat. "Don't push your luck. You have no idea what I am capable of."

"Nor you me," Enid said. "Two hundred. I'll be right back with Pepper."

TD LOOKED FROM THE OPENING to the crawl space to Lizzy. He was no fool. He could see that the lodge had settled over the years and there was no way he was going to be able to maneuver under there.

"I can do it," Lizzy said. "I've had bomb training."

He swallowed back his fear and nodded as he met her gaze. "I'll get the family out of the lodge." He wanted to say so much more, but there wasn't time. "Just be careful. And one more thing. I was hoping you'd be my date for the wedding. After all, I'm a Winchester. I would think that means I'm invited."

She laughed and shook her head. "You're that sure there's still going to be a wedding?"

"Just a little time around the Winchesters and I've learned one thing for certain. They are one tough, resilient family—and I have every faith in you that you'll find the bomb and defuse it."

Their gazes locked for a moment. "I'll see you at the wedding, then," she said and knelt down to squirm into the hole.

TD saw her disappear and, with a prayer on his lips, took off running toward the front of the lodge.

Chapter Fourteen

Lizzy crawled only a few feet under the house and stopped to listen. She held her breath, afraid Janie was under there with her. After a few moments, she heard nothing. She turned on the headlamp and shone it into the cold, cobwebbed darkness.

What she hadn't told TD was that she hated cramped spaces. Hated spiders and webs and creepy-crawly things that lived in the cold dampness beneath houses.

It stemmed back to one time when she and Janie and Anne were kids. Janie had locked her and Anne in an old root cellar on the McCormick Ranch. She remembered the smell, the cobwebs that brushed across her face and the feeling that something was crawling on her.

Forcing herself past that memory, Lizzy saw that the space under the house was even more cramped than she and TD had thought.

She barely had enough room over her head to move. She was going to have to crawl on her belly like a snake.

As Lizzy wriggled toward the first corner of the lodge, she tried to ignore the spiderwebs that hung like lace from the floorboards. Twice she had to stop to brush them from her face, trying hard not to panic as she told herself there was something down here much more scary than spiderwebs.

She stopped to catch her breath, shining the light ahead. Nothing in that corner. She turned her head. The light picked up movement. Her heart thundered in her chest as the beam caught the beady red eyes of half a dozen rats.

She shuddered as something scampered past her and had to clamp a hand over her mouth not to scream as she felt it run across her legs.

The light caught on something in the corner. Sandbags. Her pulse jumped. In the training class they'd used sandbags around bags of fertilizer. She crawled toward the corner—and the bomb.

AS TD NEARED THE LODGE, he saw no sign of Janie, but that didn't mean she wasn't still here somewhere.

He burst through the front door, then slowed. He wanted to alert everyone in the house without alerting Janie. She could decide to set off the bomb early if she knew he and Lizzy were there to stop her.

Before he could decide where to go first, he encountered Enid coming from the kitchen. "We have to get everyone out of the house now," he said and saw at once that he would have to give this old woman a reason or she would dig in her heels. "But I don't want them to panic. I believe Janie McCormick has planted a bomb under the lodge."

Enid's eyes widened. "That little bitch."

"Can you get Pepper out? Tell me where I can find the others."

"Upstairs in the north wing. Pepper's in the south wing. McCall's in a room down there, too."

"Hurry, but remember, if they panic and make a lot of noise, Janie could decide to blow the place early."

Enid nodded, but looked as if her thoughts were elsewhere as she glanced back down the hall toward the kitchen.

"Enid, forget whatever you have cooking in the kitchen. Get Pepper out of here. I want everyone to gather out front until we're sure there is no one left in the house."

"Fine," Enid said, shooting another glance toward the kitchen. She got a strange smile on her face. "Better find Pepper. She is going to be furious."

The first room TD found was Virginia's. It was early enough that no one had gotten dressed for the wedding yet.

He told Virginia what he'd told Enid, since she was another one who was too stubborn to just take his word for anything, maybe especially because he was just the cook's helper.

"Quietly get out of the house. The others are waiting for you outside."

She nodded and grabbed her coat before taking off down the hall.

Brand heard TD knocking at Worth's bedroom door. He stuck his head out of his room. "What's going on?"

"Go with Virginia. She'll tell you. We have to get everyone out of the house." He opened Worth's door. The bed was empty. A tux was laid out on the bed. He quickly checked the bathroom. Empty.

TD checked the other rooms on the wing to make sure Worth hadn't taken a different room last night.

No Worth. Where the hell was he?

JANIE HEARD THE COMMOTION out in the main lodge and realized Enid wasn't coming back with Pepper. She pushed up from the table, surprised that her legs felt like rubber. Staggering to the door, she stumbled out, almost falling. *What is wrong with me?* It came in a flash. That damned Enid. *She…she…drugged me?*

But how had the old hag even known she was coming here? She would kill Enid when she found her. She would…

Janie laughed. She wouldn't have to do anything. Once the bomb—

Realization cut through the drugged fog that was swirling in her brain. She would have to work fast now. She could feel whatever Enid had put in that coffee trying to drag her down.

Clinging to the wall, Janie worked herself around the abandoned side of the house. Behind her, she heard the front door open and the Winchesters streaming out. Someone had told them about the bomb. But they were still close enough to the house that if she could just get the fuse lit…

She reached the back corner of the house, her brain still functioning sufficiently that she congratulated herself for going with the longer fuse. She'd done that so she would have a chance to get away. Now, though…

"Time for plan B," she said to herself as

she sat down, leaning back against the side of the house next to the end of the fuse, and pulled out her satellite phone. She dialed the number, then took the lighter from her other pocket and flicked it until she had a flame.

She could feel herself slipping away. There was one person she needed to say goodbye to before she lit the fuse.

"Daddy?" she said when he answered.

"Janie, how many times have I told you not to call me that?"

She ignored his rebuke. She was about to die but she wanted him to know what a good job she'd done. She wanted him to be proud of her. "I did it."

"You took care of all of them?" he asked, sounding relieved.

"I thought you'd like to hear the bomb go off."

"Janie, I told you—"

"I had to change my plan. I had to kill Anne and burn down the house. I had to—" The rest caught in her throat as she looked up and saw Worth Winchester standing over her with a gun in his hand. "Daddy, I have to go now. I love you."

"Janie—" She dropped the phone, but held tight to the lighter as she met Worth Winchester's gaze.

"What the hell are you doing?" he asked.

Janie realized she was crying. She made a swipe at her tears with her free hand. She wished she could get to her feet, but it was too late for that. The drug had her almost immobile now. "I'm going to blow your whole family to kingdom come."

"What?" His gaze widened and then he saw the short length of fuse sticking out from under the house—and the flame of the lighter in her hand next to it. "Put that down. Now!"

She smiled. Or at least she thought she did as she touched the lighter to the fuse.

LIZZY FLINCHED AT THE SOUND of a gunshot. It had come from outside. Had TD found Janie? Or— She couldn't let herself think about that now as she crawled to the corner where Janie had left the bomb.

Behind the sandbags were two fifty-pound bags of fertilizer—just like the ones she'd seen in the shed at the McCormick Ranch. Her heart was threatening to beat out of her chest. She had to calm down and find the detonator.

She shone the flashlight around her. More eyes watching her. Making a swipe with her hand, she cleared more spiderwebs from in front of her face and tried to get up on all fours to search for the detonator.

At first it had been freezing cold under the house. Now sweat ran into her eyes. She thought of Janie dragging the sand and fertilizer bags under here—and remembered the maniacal strength the woman had had even as a girl.

Something glinted from one of the bags of fertilizer. Lizzy moved closer, all of her training making her forget the rats and the spiders as she looked for the device Janie had used that would detonate the fertilizer.

That's when she saw the line of fuse running along the wall. She followed the fuse with the headlamp down the side of the wall to an air vent where it disappeared outside at the back of the house.

She smelled it even before she saw the fuse burning. Janie had lit the fuse. It burned toward her.

Lizzy felt panic rise in her as she dragged her gaze from the burning fuse and back to the bomb. She had to find the detonator now!

TD HEARD THE GUNSHOT and froze for a second. He couldn't tell where it had come from. He listened for another and hearing none, ran down to the south wing. Again no Worth.

Who'd fired the gunshot? Lizzy? Janie? He couldn't bear to think of Lizzy down there under the house just below the floorboards and maybe not alone. Had she found the bomb? Would she be able to defuse it in time? If Janie was down there—

He shoved the thought away as he hurried downstairs. He checked to make sure everyone else had gotten out and then ran outside to where the family had gathered. He had no choice but to get the largest number of people out of danger first before he could check on Lizzy.

"Is everyone here?" he asked, knowing it wouldn't be long before more of the family would be arriving for the wedding.

"What's going on?" the sheriff demanded. She was wearing jeans and a Western shirt, but it was clear she had started fixing her hair before she'd been interrupted.

TD pulled her aside. "I'm a federal agent. I need you to stay with your family. Get them all in the vehicles and drive to the other side of the rise and keep them there. Don't let anyone else come in. Can you do that?"

"I can as soon as you tell me if what Enid told me is true," she said.

"We have reason to believe Janie McCormick planted a bomb under the lodge," he said.

"We?"

"There is another agent looking for it as we speak. Can I trust you to take command of this bunch and get them a safe distance from the house?"

She nodded and turned toward her family. "All right, everyone—"

"Where's Worth?" Brand asked as he approached them.

"Did any of you see Worth?" McCall asked, shooting a look at TD.

"I'll find him. Get the rest of these people out of there."

With that he ran back toward the lodge.

LIZZY SHONE THE LIGHT OVER the bags of fertilizer. Where was the detonator? She didn't dare look at the fuse. But out of the corner of her eye she could see it spitting out flames as it raced toward her—and the bomb.

A fuse like the one Janie had used burned at forty seconds to a foot. It seemed to be moving faster than that as she searched frantically for whatever Janie had rigged to trigger the bomb.

That's when she saw it hidden between the

sandbags. The pencil-thin two-inch silver blasting cap with the fuse stuck in one end and the other stuck in a stick of dynamite.

Her hands shaking, Lizzy reached for the blasting cap. The burning fuse was so close now that she could feel the heat. It was too late. She knew what she had to do. She jerked the fuse free of the blasting cap, rolled over on her back and threw the blasting cap as far away from her—and the bomb—as she could.

Then covered her head as it exploded.

TD HAD JUST ROUNDED the corner when he heard the boom—and saw Worth Winchester holding a gun and standing over a dead Janie McCormick. For one heart-stopping moment he waited for the second explosion, one that would level the lodge and kill them all.

But after a few seconds, he let himself breathe again. Lizzy had found the bomb and defused it. The sound, louder than a shotgun blast, was just a blasting cap going off.

He raced to the opening where he'd last seen Lizzy. He called her name and again held his breath until he heard her answer. A few moments later, she crawled to the hole and he saw her.

She was covered in dust and dirt, there

were cobwebs in her hair and tiny cuts on one cheek from when the metal blasting cap had exploded. But she'd never looked more beautiful.

He reached for her, determined not to ever let her go again.

Epilogue

The wedding of Luke Crawford and McCall Winchester was one that would be talked about for years around Whitehorse.

How many weddings, after all, required the bomb squad to be called in? Or the coroner? The day's events just added to the mysteries surrounding the infamous Winchesters.

But only a few people knew what really had happened that day out at the Winchester Ranch. One of those people was TD Waters. He'd lifted Agent Lizzy Calder out from under the lodge and carried her down to the cabin while everyone else waited for the bomb squad to arrive.

Under the hot spray of the shower, he'd held her for a long time before he'd gently peeled off her wet, dirty clothing and his own.

"Do you know what I'd like to do with you?" he asked.

She met his gaze. "Surprise me."

And he did. "I want to dance with you."

"And here I thought you had something else in mind."

"Oh, that is always on my mind when I look at you." He cupped his palms on each side of her waist and pulled her closer. "You were amazing today. You're always amazing."

Later, after they made love, he put in a call to the agency. He wasn't surprised to hear that no one could find Director Roger Collins—or a large sum of government money that had gone missing.

Meanwhile back at the ranch, Pepper Winchester had gathered her family in the lodge after the bomb squad had given the all clear. She told them a story about a sixteen-year-old girl who fell in love with a boy named Hunt McCormick years ago at a carnival, and his promise that one day he would find her and they would be together.

"Are you telling us—"

"That he found me twenty-seven years ago," Pepper said, cutting her off.

"Hunt McCormick," Worth said.

"That's why that crazy Janie McCormick tried to kill us all?" Virginia demanded.

"Virginia, the woman was just that, crazy," Brand said. "Let Mother finish. I suspect there is more to this story."

Pepper smiled at him. "Hunt and I had one wonderful night together. It resulted in a child. A son. You know him as TD Waters." She got to her feet. "I need to go find him and talk to him before the wedding. So if you'll excuse me."

"There's still going to be a wedding?" Virginia asked in shock.

"Yes," McCall said, looking over at Luke. He'd come in on foot when he'd found the road blocked by one of the ranch pickups, not all that surprised that something had happened, although while he'd worried that the wedding wouldn't go off without a hitch, he hadn't expected a bomb—or a crazy woman.

"I guess I'd better get to work, then," Enid said.

"Actually, Enid," McCall said, taking her aside. "I don't think we'll be needing you today."

"Now, just a minute..." That's when she saw the police officer outside looking at the ranch pickup with the new headlight.

"The eyewitness who saw your sister get run down remembered something else about the pickup she saw," McCall said. "The driver looked like a little old woman and there was something on the side of the truck. The words *Winchester Ranch*."

"I'll talk," Enid threatened. "I'll tell everything I know."

Pepper smiled. "Who's going to believe a woman who murdered her own sister?"

Enid didn't even put up a fight as she was led away in handcuffs. McCall was just sorry her grandmother hadn't been there to see it. But Pepper was standing outside the bunkhouse talking with TD.

TD listened to what his mother had to say, although he'd figured most of it out on his own.

"It took a long time to track you down," she told him. "Once I knew who you worked for, I knew you'd have to discover the truth on your own."

"That's why you demanded the fifty thousand dollars. If you had offered me the information for nothing, I wouldn't have believed you."

She'd smiled. "After all, you are my son."

"What do you want from me?"

"Nothing. What do you want from me?"

"Answers."

"You want to know about your father."

"Yes."

Pepper's gaze softened. "It would take a lifetime to tell you about Hunt McCormick and my love for him. I guess if you want to know the whole story you're going to have to stay around for a while."

EVERYONE SAID THE BRIDE was beautiful and so was the short but poignant ceremony. There was champagne and cake, music and dancing. The Winchester lodge was filled with a sound it hadn't heard in many, many years: laughter.

Pepper watched McCall and Luke walk out on the floor for their first dance as husband and wife. Her granddaughter had never looked more beautiful or happy and Luke Crawford was as handsome as any man could be. The love in his eyes brought tears to Pepper's.

As they began to slow dance to the music, Pepper looked around the room at her family. They were all there, her children and her grandchildren and their husbands and wives and girlfriends, some of them already pregnant, others, she suspected, not far behind. Soon she would be a great-grandmother.

What surprised her was that she liked the thought, and actually wanted to stick around for that. She realized she liked having all her family here. Worth had risked his life today. Call would have been proud.

Pepper had even been surprised by her reaction to Trace's widow, Ruby. The woman would never have been her first choice for her son, but Ruby was McCall's mother and that alone made her family. And clearly Ruby was in love with Red Harper, Pepper thought as she watched the two dance. After all these years, Ruby and Trace's best friend, Red, were finally moving on.

Pepper felt her heart swell with love for this family of hers. Maybe someday they would forgive her. Maybe they had already started.

TD held Lizzy close as they danced. Pepper had lent her a dress from a closet full of vintage clothing. He looked into her eyes. "I love you, Lizzy Calder."

She smiled up at him. "I wondered how long it would take you to realize that." She rose on her tiptoes and kissed him as music played around them to the clink of champagne glasses and the soft roar of a fire in the huge rock fireplace.

TD had said he didn't know what he would do now that they'd decided their lives as agents were behind them. But Lizzy had seen him look out across the wild prairie, across this immense Winchester Ranch, and she'd seen their future as clear and bright as the December day.

Just when the wedding couldn't have been more perfect, it began to snow. Huge lacy flakes drifted down from a midnight-blue sky and everyone ran to the window to watch. They were going to have a white Christmas.

The day's events would have been sufficient for the local gossips to feast on for months, but it was what happened next that would have people talking for years.

No one heard the knock at the door over the music. Few even turned when the door opened on a gust of wind.

But Pepper Winchester did. She turned to find Hunt McCormick standing framed in the doorway as if some part of her had known.

She felt her heart fill with helium at the sight of him.

"May I have this dance?" he asked. He couldn't have looked more handsome in his tuxedo. He was smiling down at her.

As he drew her to her feet, she said, "I'm not sure I remember how to dance."

"As long as I can hold you in my arms, I don't care how much dancing we do," he said and drew her into his embrace.

She closed her eyes as she put her cheek against his shoulder, and it was as if they were young again, their lives stretched out before them with so many possibilities.

"I have something I've wanted to give you for years," Hunt said reaching into his pocket as the song ended. He pulled out a gold chain with a heart locket. It glittered with diamonds.

Pepper felt tears well in her eyes. He'd promised years ago to replace a cheap heart locket he'd given her—the same locket she'd put on the small grave up on the hill that she'd always known had never held hers and Hurt's son.

He clasped the chain, then stepped back to look at her, love in his eyes.

"Run away with me," Hunt whispered. "And don't tell me it's too late."

Pepper lifted her face to his. "No, not too late, but I'm through running away. Stay with me, Hunt. Stay here with me and my family on this ranch. There is still time, isn't there?"

He looked down into her eyes, tears welling in his. "Whatever time we have, I want it to be together."

She smiled up at him. "There is so much I need to tell you."

"Tomorrow," he said. "Tonight, I just want to dance."

But as they danced, her gaze caught on her daughter. Virginia held up her champagne glass as if in a silent toast, and Pepper knew that Virginia had called Hunt and, knowing her daughter, probably told him everything. And yet he was here.

She smiled her thanks and then closed her eyes as she danced with the man she loved as if all those years had never passed.

* * * * *